All My Love, Martin

A Story of Friendship, Love and War

By

Julie D'Olympio

Chapter One

June 15, 1995

D ressed in his flight suit, Martin rushed into the emergency room waiting area of the Beaufort Naval Hospital. He couldn't believe what was going on. All around the room, nurses were scurrying about. A doctor was standing outside a room. He looked up and saw Martin, then motioned for him to come over. The doctor was looking at a medical chart. Doctor Peterson was a handsome man with salt and pepper hair. He had rugged features, but a gentle disposition. He was usually full of smiles, always one to bring other people's spirits up, but this time, he looked somber.

This was definitely not the time for smiles. Doctor Peterson was Diana's physician when she was younger, and although the doctor hadn't seen her for several years, he was well aware of her medical condition.

Martin was beginning to panic. Diana was his best friend in the world. Although he had nothing but respect for the doctor, he was close to grabbing him and shaking him if he didn't tell him what was going on with her. She had an asthma attack. That was all Martin knew. She had had many small attacks before, but only one other was this bad. Just like then, Martin was afraid he was going to lose her. Just like before, this one came on unexpected. One minute, she was fine, watching him flying his jet at the air show while she chatted with LeAnne and Katherine. The next, she was rushed to the hospital, unable to breathe properly.

After Martin landed, he had driven to the hospital, praying the whole way. Upon arriving in the ER, he had rushed to the receptionist desk yelling for someone to tell him how Diana was doing and where they took her. All too quickly, she had been whisked away by nurses and Martin was stopped to fill out paperwork on her. The elderly receptionist at the front desk was asking him questions about her medical history and health insurance. He didn't want to answer questions; he wanted to be with her. He wanted to make sure she was okay. After an agonizing wait, Dr. Peterson finally spoke up.

"Martin, she's gone into premature labor. We need to try to stop the contractions. She's only twenty-eight weeks along. Dr. Hines, the OB on call is checking on her and the baby's condition. The doctor put his hand on Martin's shoulder to add comfort.

"You might want to call any of her family members. Let them know. I won't lie to you, Martin. Her situation is critical. We have to be careful here."

"Can I see her now? I need to be with her!" Martin was concerned, and his worries were growing by the second.

"You'll get to see her soon, I promise." Dr. Peterson knew Martin was near panic, and tried his best to calm him down.

"Right now, she's in good hands. We'll keep you informed as often as we can." Martin just nodded his head. He felt like crying and yelling at the same time. She had to be okay. She was his world, his life, his every breath. But right at that moment, his world was in a room somewhere gasping for air. She needed him and he needed to be with her. He felt helpless. The room started spinning. All the people in the waiting area around him seemed surreal. They appeared to be mere shadows. He saw a woman sitting with her sick baby trying to comfort it. To Martin they seemed like ghosts, or just part of a terrible bad dream. He wondered if soon they would disappear and he would wake up, all of this being only a dream. Suddenly a nurse came rushing out of a room and whispered something to Dr. Peterson. Dr. Peterson looked concerned. Martin knew that wasn't good. The doctor looked up at Martin and spoke.

"Diana's is in distress so they are taking her in to do an emergency cesarean. They're going to have to deliver. I'm sorry but you'll have to wait out here. I'll keep you posted on her condition." Martin wanted desperately to know what the nurse had said. How was she? Why couldn't he go in and see her? She needed him and he needed her. The nurse who had whispered to the Doctor now turned to Martin and spoke.

"We have a Chaplain down in the hospital's Chapel. If you'd like, I will send for him." Martin let out a gasp.

"Oh God!" He almost fell to his knees. It took all his strength to keep from falling over sobbing. Dr. Peterson turned to the nurse with a scowl.

"Candace, this is not the time!" Quickly the nurse stepped back with her head down, and then quickly returned to the room where she had emerged. Dr. Peterson turned back towards Martin and put his hand on his shoulder.

"She didn't mean to imply anything regarding her and the child's condition, only to offer support. In times like these, it's always nice to have someone to talk to. Martin, we will do the very best we can to help her and the baby. Now I must go in and assist Dr. Hines. I will let you know something as soon as I find out, I promise." Martin looked up at him. All Martin could do right then was just nod, put his trust in God and the medical team. The doctor saw desperation in his eyes. He felt sorry for Martin. He knew how she meant the world to him. With all the commotion, she had been rushed to the elevator and off to the third floor for surgery before Martin could even see, much less speak to her. As Dr Peterson turned and walked off, Martin knew he needed to make a phone call. He started patting for pockets but then quickly realized he was in his flight suit and did not have any change for a pay phone. He had to call her family. They had to know what was going on. He didn't want to be going through all this alone. He walked over and asked the receptionist where the closest complementary phone was. She looked up from her paperwork and pointed down the hall.

"Straight down the hall, last room on the left. Dial nine for outside calls." she said. He thanked her and headed that way. The first person he called was her parents in New York. The phone rang three times before James picked up.

"Hello" answered James.

"James, this is Martin." He hesitated for a moment.

"We were at the air show here in Beaufort when Diana started having an asthma attack. We're at the Naval Hospital right now"

"Oh God! How is she and the baby?" Martin let out a sigh.

"I wish I knew. They won't let me in with her." Martin coughed to collect his composure somewhat.

"They're doing an emergency cesarean right now." He was trying to hold back from crying but wasn't succeeding, as his eyes welled up.

"The doctors are doing what they can, but you two should probably come down." There was silence on the other line for a few seconds.

"Of course! Nancy and I will make the flight arrangements and we'll be there as soon as we can. Hang in there Martin, we're on the way." Martin hung up and slowly walked toward the waiting room. Just then his mother showed up. He felt a bit of relief when he saw her.

"Mom, I'm glad you're here!" She put her hand in his.

"Of course, I came right away when Katherine called. How is she doing?"

"The asthma attack brought on contractions. They were going to try to stop the contractions but she suddenly went into distress. They're doing an emergency cesarean. I don't know much because they won't let me see her." His voice cracked along with his composure.

"Oh God Mom, what am I going to do if I lose her?" He began crying. After a few seconds of silence, she spoke up.

"You just stay calm. I'm sure she'll be fine. God knows how much you two need each other. I doubt He's about to take her away from you just yet. I know she and the baby will be okay, you understand?" She waited for him to respond.

"Okay, he choked."

"Good. Hang in there." He just nodded.

"I'm going to see if I can find out anything since I work here and they know me. I'll be right back." Teresa walked over to the desk. Martin just stood there thinking. This all had to be a dream. He wasn't really there at the hospital. This wasn't real. This all couldn't be happening. He was just having trouble waking up, but this wasn't a dream. It was cold hard reality right in his face. He wasn't going to just stand around waiting, not knowing.

Over at the information desk, Teresa was arguing with the lady at the desk about rules and regulations. Martin decided he was going to somehow get in and see her. He looked over at the elevator, but it was up on the 8th floor and he didn't have time to wait. He headed for the stairs. Once he made it to the third floor, he did his best to not be seen. Looking around, he wasn't sure where to go. But then he saw a sign for the OR. He noticed that you needed a badge to get in there. Just as he was trying to figure out his next move, a group of nurses walked by. He quickly hid behind a corner until they passed. One of them used their badge to open the door for the OR area. They all went in and just before the door closed completely, Martin grabbed it, pulled it open and went in unseen.

Once inside, he immediately saw a shelf full of blankets. He ducked behind it. He wasn't sure how he was going to get to Diana without being seen. He started looking on the shelf for a lab coat. There were none, but he looked off to the right of the shelf and saw a basket of dirty laundry. He rummaged through it and almost immediately he found what he needed. Quickly he put on the lab coat. It wasn't very clean but it would at least make him less conspicuous. A couple of nurses walked by, but did not pay attention to him. He had gone unnoticed.

Now he needed to find out where she was. He passed a room but it was empty. He heard voices behind him and he quickly ducked inside. The lights were out, so he was not seen. After a moment of hiding behind the wall, he heard the sound of a cry. A baby was crying! Martin slowly peaked around the doorway and saw an incubator being wheeled out of the operating room and toward a waiting elevator. He knew it was her room, and that was Diana's baby. His heart began to melt. He wanted to run over and scoop up the child, but he had to stay unseen, at least until he saw her. He would have to wait until he had a clear shot of the door.

He waited for the right moment and finally, when the coast was clear, he made a dash to the door. But just as he got there, it opened. He quickly ducked behind the door as it came open. Another nurse was coming out. As she walked away, he quickly peaked in.

Inside the Operating room he saw the two doctors above her bed. Nurses were walking around retrieving things for the doctors. He couldn't see Diana because her bed was crowded by the medical team. Only her left hand was in view. He was overcome with emotion and worry. He wanted to be happy about the baby. He wanted to see her sit up and smile over at him, let him know she was okay. He wanted desperately to believe in his heart that she was going to be fine, but he knew that bad things happen.

When you least expect it, life as you know it can be turned upside down in an instant, leaving you devastated and desperate for a reason. She was the best thing that ever happened to him. Suddenly, a long beep came from a machine she was hooked up to. His mind was flooded with fear and emotion. They were overpowering him. He couldn't move or breathe as he heard a nurse yell,

"Her blood pressure is dropping! We're losing her!"

Chapter Two

June 7, 1981

(14 years earlier)

It was hot and muggy. Martin wasn't at all in a good mood as his mother's red van pulled in through the base gate. He didn't want to move away. He was perfectly content in their old home at Camp Pendleton in California. His mother had gotten a transfer to the Marine Corps base in Beaufort, South Carolina and Martin wasn't a willing participant in the matter. His mom stopped at the checkpoint and showed the

Military Police officer her I.D. The man smiled, winked and signaled her to drive through. Teresa was a strikingly attractive woman. Even wearing camo with her long blond hair pulled back in a bun, she could turn a man's head. The M.P. was no exception. Martin sat in the passenger seat staring forward. The base was no different than the last one. Nothing special to see.

"Why do we have to move in the first place? All my friends are back in San Diego." His mom looked at him and gave him a half smile.

"We went over this hundreds of times. We needed a change since your father died. I can't be there without him. It's just too painful for me. When you get older, you'll understand." He rolled his eyes and let out a sigh as his mother continued.

"Besides, this gives you a chance to make new friends and it gives us both a chance to make a fresh start; to get past the pain." She stopped talking for a few seconds to fight back tears. She knew this was hard on him but she couldn't hide her pain very well, although she tried her best to be strong in front of her son. I don't want a fresh start. This wasn't my idea.

Besides, they probably don't have anything to do here. Probably never even heard of a movie theater."

"Very funny mister. Now look, this is our new home. We have to make the best of it." His mom seemed like she was trying to convince herself of the fact as well.

"This isn't easy for me either. I hate starting a job at a new site, but we'll get through this, wait and see." She reached over and rubbed his shoulder and gave him a smile. She knew it was hard on him to leave his school and friends behind. Teresa felt bad about it, but she just couldn't stay there in San Diego. It was too painful to stay there with Steve's memory. It was hard putting on a brave front for Martin, but she had to. It had been two months since the accident and healing from the pain of it would be a long process.

One she knew she could never get through if she stayed there where his memory was everywhere she turned. To her, getting away was her only hope of continuing to function in a shattered world. Maybe it would hurt less somewhere else where they didn't share memories.

"They have a great school on base and when you graduate, Paris Island is just down the road for you to go for basic training." Martin wanted to be a pilot in the Marine Corps like his father. He was a little excited about being near where his father went through boot camp. To Martin, his father was a hero he wanted to be like. Teresa was afraid that his dreams of being a pilot like his father were wiped out with his father's death, but it made him want even more to be a pilot. He wanted to follow in his dad's footsteps and make him proud. Martin tapped his fingers on the glass of the passenger window.

"This just isn't fair." As they pulled into a neighborhood, he noticed some kids about his age playing baseball in a field behind some houses. He wondered if they would end up being his new friends. He knew it would be hard being the new kid in the neighborhood. The car pulled into the driveway of the fifth house on the right.

"Here we are, #708." his mom said with excitement. As the car came to a stop, Martin noticed the house was smaller than their old base housing, but it was just the two of them now. A bigger house wasn't needed. Already parked in the driveway was a blue truck.

"Looks like the housing lady is already here to let us in. It doesn't seem so bad. What do you say we go in and see if it's just as nice inside?"

"Base housing is never really nice Mom. Why couldn't we live out in town?" Teresa sighed.

"I couldn't find anything on such short notice. Now come on. Let's go check out the place." Martin gave her a "do we have to" look and got out of the car. Teresa went to the front door and knocked twice. Martin was walking slowly, watching the kids playing baseball in the field behind his house. He wished he could join in. Baseball was his favorite sport. Back in San Diego, he was the best on his team. The door to their new house opened and a tall attractive Hispanic lady stood in the doorway.

"You must be the Davises. Come in and we'll get started with the tour." Teresa and Martin entered and the lady led them to the kitchen. The house was small, and the kitchen was not much bigger than a walk-in closet.

"By the way, I'm Mattie Richardson. You'll be dealing directly with me for any housing problems you may have. The base houses here are fairly new so there shouldn't be that many problems. Now take a look around and make sure all the windows open and close, all the cabinets are top notch and everything is in working order. I have some paperwork I need you to sign when you're done."

"Thanks." Teresa gave Mattie a smile and she started looking around. Martin followed behind his mother. They looked around the kitchen and Teresa opened all the cabinets and turned on and off the faucets.

"Water runs." Then she walked back to the bathroom and did the same in there. She entered the first bedroom. It was a pretty decent size. It had a walk-in closet. The window faced out in the backyard field where the kids were playing baseball.

"It seems like a nice room." Teresa said. Then they walked into the other bedroom. It was the same size as the first, also with a walk-in closet, but this room had two windows. One faced the backfield like the first bedroom, but the other window faced the house next door. Martin slowly walked to the window facing the ball field and watched the kids playing ball. He was suddenly looking out at a memory of him and his father throwing a baseball back and forth. Martin was about seven then. He could hear in his head his father's voice…

"Okay now Martin, you are about to experience an all-time record of the fastest pitch thrown by a dad." Martin laughed.

"Okay Dad but don't make it too fast or I won't be able to catch it." His dad chuckled.

"I promise Martin, I won't throw you anything I know you can't handle. Now get ready, here it comes." His dad threw the ball fast, but not too fast for Martin. Martin was able to catch it. His dad praised him.

"Great catch. You see? I will always keep my promise to you. I love you son."

"I love you too, Dad!" Martin's memory was interrupted by his mother entering the room behind him.

"What do you think about this room?"

"I'll take this room." said Martin. He liked the extra window. He had a funny feeling that he was supposed to choose that room. Teresa sensed that her son's thoughts were far away.

"You okay?" He turned to her with a half-smile and said

"Sure. Just really missing him, you know?" Teresa put her arm around his shoulders.

"Yes, I do know. So, what do you think?" Martin looked back out at the kids in the ball field.

"I guess I can give it a try." Teresa smiled.

"Good. That's all I ask. Now let's go see Mattie and fill out the paperwork on our new home." After they had inspected the house, they went back in the kitchen where Mattie was waiting for them.

"We'll take it." said Teresa.

"Good, now please sign these forms and you'll be ready to move in. Do you have your belongings stored here on base?"

"Yes, I meant to ask you where I go to get them." Mattie fumbled through the paperwork and handed her a piece of paper.

"Here. Just call this number and let them know you're ready for your belongings to be delivered. They usually are pretty good at getting your stuff to you the next day.

"Thanks." Teresa took the paper and put it by the phone. She signed the paperwork that read everything was in proper working condition.

"Now here on page five are the housing rules. Read and follow them carefully. I wouldn't want you nice people to get kicked out for not following them. They're really strict on rules here. They consider it a privilege for you to live here on base. It's just the two of you, right?" Teresa lowered her head.

"Yes, that's right."

"I heard about your loss. I'm so sorry." Mattie put her hand on Teresa's shoulder to comfort her. Teresa gave a tiny smile.

"Thanks. It's been tough. I was asked if I wanted a hardship discharge but I love the Corps. I wouldn't want to leave it. It's all I know." Mattie gave her a smile and said, "My husband is a gung-ho Marine. I don't think there is anything that would keep him away from his job either. He's a Staff Sergeant. He's been in his squadron for seven years and loves it. He's a little hard on the boys but they need that from time to time. Your husband, he was a pilot, wasn't he?"

"Yes, he was.

Martin was crazy about his father. In fact, he wants to be a pilot just like him." Mattie smiled down at Martin and gave him a quick pat on the shoulder.

"Really! Following in your dad's footsteps, huh? I hope that works out for you Martin. And from what I hear, pilots have no problem with the ladies." Martin blushed at the thought. He hadn't really paid girls much attention yet. The girls he went to school with in San Diego were self-centered and snobby. Mattie turned back to Teresa.

"Well, if everything seems fine, I'll be going. Here are your keys. If you have any questions, my number is on the top of page one. Enjoy your new home."

"Thanks," Teresa said. She walked Mattie to the door.

"Remember to read the rules. Oh! And welcome to Beaufort." Teresa and Mattie waved bye and Teresa shut the door. Martin was leaning on the counter, trying to take it all in. Moving was hard on him. He wasn't used to it. He had lived in the same house on base back in San Diego all his life. He felt lost and alone. Teresa looked up at him and slapped her hands together.

"Well, what do you say we order a pizza? I bet you're starving." Martin was. They hadn't had a bite to eat since lunch at a drive-in restaurant hours ago. Teresa found a phone book on top of the refrigerator and located a pizza restaurant that delivers. As she called the order in, Martin went to the car and got his duffle bag out of the trunk. He could hear laughter from the kids playing baseball back in the field behind the houses and looked up to watch. He hoped that they would accept him into their little group.

Being the new kid was going to be tough enough, but making friends could be even tougher. They looked like they were having fun. He thought about going over and introducing himself, but decided against it. He went back inside and took his bag to his new room. He took out his electronic hand-held baseball game and sat on the floor. He played his game until the pizza deliveryman showed up.

Moments later, his mom called to him to come eat, so he turned off his game and went into the kitchen, still holding it. Since they didn't yet have their furniture, his mom had set a place to eat on the living room floor with paper plates and the pizza box.

"I put the soda cans in the freezer for a few minutes to get cold. Just grab one if you want." His mom was sitting on the floor, eating a piece of pizza. He grabbed a soda from the freezer and went to sit down beside her. As they ate, Teresa started talking about her new job, and how things were going to be much better in their new home. Martin didn't say much. He was still upset with her for making him move away from his friends. When they finished eating, he threw his plate away and took his soda and game out onto the porch while Teresa phoned her friend Misty from back in San Diego to tell her about the trip and their new home. It was getting dark and the kid's baseball game had ended. No kids were in sight. They had all probably been called in for dinner by now, he thought. began to play his game.

Just then, he heard a voice, a very beautiful voice in the distance. Somewhere, a young girl was singing. It was the most beautiful voice he had ever heard. It sounded like an angel to him. It was coming from somewhere around him. The song sounded familiar to him, but he couldn't remember the name. It was a song he had heard in church several times. He put down his game and stood up. He wanted to see where that voice was coming from.

Curiosity got the best of him and so he followed the sound. It led to the house next door. It had gotten dark outside and it was difficult for him to see, but he made his way to the yard next door. A window was open and a light was on inside. He could hear the voice coming from inside the open window behind a curtain. He crept over to the open window and peeked inside, careful not to be seen.

Inside, he saw a man playing the piano while a young girl standing beside him was singing. It must be her father, he thought. The man looked up from the keys and smiled up at the girl. She stood with her back towards the window as she sang, but as she soon turned around, he saw her! He caught his breath. She was even more beautiful than her voice. She looked to be about his age. She was wearing a white dress. Her hair was long and auburn. He couldn't take his eyes off her. She had a natural beauty about her, not like the girls back in California, who wore way too much make-up. She didn't look like she had a drop of make-up on. He just stood there and listened to her voice. He closed his eyes for just a second to enjoy the music. The song took him back to a memory of going to church with his dad and mom, before the accident; a time when he felt so safe and secure.

Strangely, he felt safe and secure listening to her sing. He couldn't tell if it was just the memory of his father, or something more. He was mysteriously drawn to her voice, like a lost wanderer in the wilderness is drawn to the sound of a cool spring. All of a sudden, she stopped singing. Martin was so wrapped up in his thoughts that he didn't realize at first. A few seconds later, her dad stopped playing. Martin's eyes popped open.

"What's the matter, honey?" the man asked her. She pointed over to the window where Martin was standing. He quickly ducked down; afraid he'd been spotted for sure.

"Daddy, someone was right there out the window watching me." She said. Her father got up and went over to the window and looked out. It was dark out and he couldn't see much. Luckily, Martin went unseen by her father as he stood off to the side of the window against the house; standing perfectly still as to not be seen.

"I don't see anyone. It must have been a cat or something."

"But I saw him right out there looking at me." He looked out again.

"I don't see anything honey. But if it makes you feel better, I'll close the blinds." She nodded her head and he walked over to the window and pulled down the blinds. Martin let out a sigh and ran back to his porch. She had seen him spying on her. He grabbed up his game and soda from his front steps and ran into his house; closing the door behind him.

Inside, his mother was still on the phone talking to her friend Misty. He ran right by her and went to his room and closed the door. Teresa gave a concerned look. He was acting weird. But lately, since his father's death, that was normal. Inside his room, he opened his window, hoping he could get a faint sound of her singing. He could hear her again. He lay down in the sleeping bag his mom had laid out on the floor for him. He just lay there looking up at the ceiling, soaking in her beautiful voice, feeling comfort. A moment later, light from the hallway filled the room. His mother walked in.

"Are you feeling alright, Martin?" He looked over to where she was standing.

"Sure, just tired. I thought I would turn in early."

"That sounds like a good idea. We need to get an early start tomorrow getting settled in. They're going to deliver our stuff about 9 am and it'll take half the day to unpack. You get a good night's sleep."

"I'll try." She blew him a kiss and closed the door. The room was dark again. As he lay there, he thought about the auburn-haired girl. He didn't know her name, but she was the most beautiful girl he had ever seen. Even more so than the fake girls in California he grew up with. He drifted off to sleep listening to her angelic voice. It seemed his interest in girls had just begun.

Chapter Three

The furniture arrived the next day. Martin was up bright and early in his room unpacking. As he was looking through boxes, he came across his father's picture. He stood holding it for a moment, just looking. His father's death had hit him pretty hard and he was still unable to see his father's pictures without almost breaking down. He placed it on his night stand and just stared at it for a minute. He was remembering the night his father left for the deployment to Italy.   He sat and watched his father pack. Martin was sad and not talking much. He didn't want his dad going so far away for six months. His father was putting shirts in a bag when he looked over at Martin, sitting silently on the edge of the bed. His father spoke up.

"You're a young man now. You'll be the man of the house while I'm gone. Your mom will really need the extra help around the house. You'll do fine."

"But six months is such a long time." Martin interrupted.

"Flying can be dangerous. Plus, Dad, what if…." His dad cut his words off.

"Now don't think bad things son. Everything will be fine. Just keep thinking of the good times we will have when I return. We'll take that fishing trip we've been talking about for a while now. These six months will fly by pretty fast, what with school and your baseball games. It'll be over before you know it. And I plan on bringing you back a surprise." Martin's face lit up a little.

"Will you take me up on your jet?" Martin was excited about the idea of that. He wanted to be a pilot like his dad, and loved jets. He dreamed of flying with his dad someday. His dad was a hero to him. He was liked by all, and never knew anyone who didn't enjoy his company. Martin held onto his father's words like it was the most important thing in the world, and to Martin it was.

For almost six long months, he would rush home after baseball practice each day to see if there was a letter, or a message on the answering machine from his dad. Most days there was, but he knew that his dad wasn't always in an area where he could easily make a call, or send out a letter. Martin didn't mind, as long as his father did what he could to call them. Then the day came that Martin had been waiting a long, hard six months for. His dad was coming home. He was, after a few stops on the way, to arrive back in California, to his awaiting wife and son. Martin barely got any sleep the night before. Thoughts of hugging him, and going with him on that fishing trip that they both had talked about for so long, were flooding his mind. He got up early that morning, and waited. His mom kept herself busy with house work and cooking, but Martin was just too antsy and as the hours began to tick by, he began to get a little worried.

"He'll be back soon, just probably caught up somewhere refueling or something." She told him. But the worry could not be hidden from her son through her own eyes. She was beginning to worry herself as it got late. Then around midnight, there was a knock on the door. Martin rushed to open the door expecting to see his dad holding out his arms for a hug; instead, he saw his aunt Becky standing by a man dressed in military uniform, along with the base Chaplain. They asked for Teresa. Slowly and without a word she walked towards the door, but her legs gave way and she ended up sinking down to the floor on her knees. She knew what their arrival meant and she just sat on the floor.

"Not him, Oh God, not him."

"Mrs. Davis?" Without looking up she whispered a weak "yes." Then they gave her the devastating news. Martin had blacked out some of the memory but from what he could remember of the details, the officer explained that his father had been flying his jet back to base when his plane went down. He was missing. Aunt Becky had rushed over and held her sister.

Martin just stood there yelling, "It's not true! You're lying!" But it was the horrible truth. The next day, the wreckage was found. Days went by before

Martin stopped crying. It was very hard on them both, but when Martin was still having trouble adjusting to life at home without his dad, that's when Teresa decided to put in for a transfer. She wanted to get him away from that place, with all the memories of his father. Martin shook the painful memory of that night from his mind. He continued to unpack. He came across his baseball cap and glove. He picked them up and went over to the window.

Outside in the field, the kids were playing another game of baseball. He wanted to go join them, but would they accept him? He needed to do it. He needed to make friends to get settled in his new home. He got up the nerve and decided to see if he could play. As he passed his mother who was unpacking kitchen items, he told her he was going to watch the game outside. She told him to be careful, as she always did, and he headed outside. It was hot and humid out. The air was thick with moisture. He almost changed his mind. He wasn't used to this kind of weather.

In California, it was hot but it was a dry heat. He went around the corner of his house and headed for the field. There were more kids out playing than the day before. He got closer and took a deep breath. It was hard being the new kid. Something he was not used to. As he got closer to them, the kid who was the pitcher stopped and looked up at Martin. All the other kids looked up to see what he was looking at. Martin felt like running away but just stood there. The pitcher motioned for Martin to come over. He got nervous but walked towards the boy. As he approached him, the kid took off his baseball cap.

"I ain't seen you around here before. You must be the one who moved in that house over there." pointing to Martin's house.

"That's right." said Martin. The kid at bat was getting anxious to play.

"Well, are we going to play or what?" the batter said. The pitcher held out his hand to Martin.

"I'm Mike. Welcome to the neighborhood. There's not much around here to do, so we usually play baseball all summer. That and swimming at the lake." Martin shook his hand.

"Thanks, I'm Martin." Acceptance. Martin felt a world of relief. His first friend. Mike spoke up again.

"This field ain't much, but we put in a game once or twice a day. Like I said, there's not much else to do around here, ya know? You're welcome to join us, if you like." Sure, why not?" Martin said with a smile. The batter was getting even more uptight.

"Well, are you two going to hug, or are we going to play some ball?" The other kids laughed.

"Don't get your jockey shorts in a wad, Randy." Mike shouted back. Mike turned back to Martin and asked if he played baseball.

"Yep, I played on the school team back in California."

"California? Boy are you a long way from home. Well Good! You're up next at bat. Go over and practice your swing." Martin walked over to the extra bats and picked up one and began to practice swinging. Some girls who were sitting behind him were giggling. It made him nervous. He thought maybe they were giggling at him. Mike threw a pitch and Randy hit it. It went way up in the air and he took off running. He made it to second base and stopped safe. Then it was Martin's turn. After a few practice swings, Martin walked up to the plate. He practiced one or two more swings. Mike yelled out, "Hey everyone, this is Martin, the new kid from California. Everyone cut him some slack. He's seems pretty cool." Mike gave him a smile. Martin smiled back.

"Okay, let's play some ball!" Mike wound up his arm and threw the ball. Martin swung but missed.

"Strike!" yelled the female catcher under the mask. That voice seemed familiar to Martin somehow. The kid Randy on second base yelled out a remark.

"You swing like a baby. Do they not know how to play real ball in California?" More giggles.

"Don't pay attention to him, Martin. Randy's a jerk!" the catcher behind him said. Martin turned around and saw the face between the bars on the catcher's mask. It was a girl. She was the girl from the night before. The angel with such a pretty face and voice. He was surprised to see such a soft, delicate looking female playing catcher in a baseball game. She looked up at Martin and gave him a smile. He smiled back.

"Careful, Mike strikes everyone out the first time." Time for him to make a good impression on her. He had to make a home run.

"Thanks for the warning." He winked and turned back to face the field. He swung the bat for practice a few times and got his stance ready. Mike threw another pitch. Martin swung with all his might. Crack! The ball flew far into the air. All the kids stood with their faces towards the sky watching the ball sail far away.

"Holy Cow!" yelled Randy as he started rounding the bases. Martin tipped his hat at the giggly girls, dropped the bat and took off running as fast as he could. He reached first base, then second.

"Run!" The angel was yelling. He ran harder and harder. Randy ran home and dropped on the ground. The kid in left field went for the ball that had landed in the woods. Martin slowed down as he came into home. All the kids were cheering for him. So was the angel. He felt so proud. The kid in left field was still searching for the ball as everyone came and crowded around Martin.

"You're alright!" said Randy. "Thanks, but I was just getting warmed up." He was having a great time. He was glad he had decided to try to join their game. They continued to play and this time, Martin played third base. They played for hours. He looked down at his watch and realized his mom would have lunch waiting for him. He had worked up an appetite out in the heat. He waved goodbye to his new friends and headed home. As he was walking away, he turned and looked at the angel. She waved goodbye to him and smiled. He smiled back. For the first time since they left San Diego, he was glad they had moved. Inside the house, Teresa was making sandwiches. As he walked in, she greeted him with a smile. She noticed he was smiling for the first time since his father died. She was glad that he had come around. He saw she was smiling at him.

"What?" He hadn't realized that it was the first time he had smiled in a long time.

"I'm just glad to see that you seem happy."

"Oh."

"I saw you out there playing ball with the other kids. Do they seem nice?" He grabbed a sandwich and a soda and sat down at the table.

"Yep, they're alright."

"Good. By the way, my leave ends tomorrow. I thought we could do something tonight. They have a movie theater on base. Would you like to go?" Martin liked that idea.

"So, they've actually heard of movie theaters around here?" he asked with a little playful sarcasm. She just gave him a look.

"So, what's playing, anyway?"

"Just that new sci fi movie you've been dying to see." she answered with a smile. He finished his bite.

"Cool." After they ate, he went to take a shower. He got dressed and waited for his mom to get ready. He turned on the TV to see what was on. It was a documentary about jets. He watched and listened. If he was going to be a pilot, he thought he had better find out all he can. After a few minutes, his mom walked in the room. Seeing what Martin was watching, she giggled.

"Great! Now I'll never get you out of the house." He looked up.

"Very funny." She grabbed her purse.

"Come on, we'll be late if we don't get there in 10 minutes."   He turned off the TV and they headed out. The line for the movie tickets was long. It seemed like just about everyone on base was there to see the movie. Martin was looking up, reading the movie title on the sign. He had wanted to see it for a long time. All of a sudden, he heard a man's voice.

"Teresa, I thought that was you." Martin turned and saw a man that looked familiar to him.

"James, Hi! I want you to meet my son, Martin. I told you about him when you came over earlier to help me move some boxes."

"Oh, yes I remember." The man held out his hand for Martin to shake.

"Martin, this is James Taylor from next door." said Teresa. They shook hands.

"It's nice to meet you, Martin." James looked familiar but Martin couldn't place where he had seen him before.   Martin shook his hand and said "You too." Teresa spoke up.

"And this must be your daughter, Diana, who you told me about." Martin hadn't noticed a girl standing behind James. He was a tall man.

"Oh yes, this is my daughter, Diana." An auburn-haired girl appeared from behind James. Martin's heart skipped a beat. It was her. The angel from the ballgame, and from the window the night before.

"We met today, already." she said with a smile. He finally knew her name. Diana. He thought that was the prettiest name he had ever heard. She had a blue dress on. She looked wonderful, he thought to himself. It sure is a small world, he thought. The line moved and they all made their way in.

"Why don't the two of you come sit with the two of us?" asked James.

"We would love to, wouldn't we?" asked Teresa. Martin and Diana stood there smiling at each other.

"Sure." he said. He liked that idea. James and Teresa sat down together and Martin and Diana sat down beside them. Martin felt a little nervous sitting there next to her. He could tell she was a little nervous too. James and Teresa soon left to get them all popcorn and soda. Then, he really felt tense. He wanted to talk to her but didn't know what to say. All around them were muffled voices of people talking softly before the movie would start. He had never been on a date, but he figured it must be just as awkward trying to find something to talk about.

"You're a good hitter," she finally said.

"So, you're from California, huh?" She was talking to him. He cleared his throat.

"Yes, from Camp Pendleton near San Diego."

"My mom lives in San Francisco. She knows lots of famous people. Have you ever seen a famous person?"

"I once saw Bob Richter at a mall."

"Who's Bob Richter?" she asked. Martin shifted his body to be facing her more.

"Oh, he was from that 70's space show that comes on Channel seven each evening. He was the captain."

"Oh, I know that show. My dad loves it."

"My dad loves, I mean loved that show too." He lowered his head a little thinking about his dad. He had trouble remembering to talk about his dad in the past tense.

"It's not every day a girl plays catcher." he said, trying to keep the conversation going.

"Well, it's the only position my dad will let me play." She explained.

"I have asthma and sometimes it gets pretty bad. My dad worries too much so I'm not really supposed to run or anything like that."

"Oh" said Martin. They smiled at each other. Just then Teresa and James returned with their treats. Soon after, the movie started. Martin and Diana shared popcorn and an occasional smile throughout the scenes. He enjoyed the movie. He noticed Diana was getting a little bit sleepy. The thought of putting his arm around her entered his mind but he didn't attempt it. After the movie, James invited them out for ice cream at a place off base. While they sat and ate their frozen treats, Martin noticed his mom was flirting quite a bit with James. It made Martin feel uneasy to see his mom acting that way with someone else besides his dad. She must have sensed what he was thinking because she looked over at him and her smile slowly faded Later, that evening, when he and Teresa got home, she came into his room to talk. She sat down on his bed next to him as he played his hand-held game.

"I noticed you seemed a bit unnerved when we were eating ice cream. Do you want to talk about it?" He looked up from his game.

"It just bothered me the way you were acting with James. I'm not used to you being friendly to other guys, that's all."

"Oh," she said. She understood that it must have been weird to him to see his mom have a guy friend. She let out a sigh and put her arm around him.

"Martin, you know how much I loved your father, more than any wife ever loved her husband. His death was the worst thing I have ever been through in my entire life. I know you're a little too young right now to understand this, but sometimes it takes friendships in your life to help you get over the pain of losing someone. James is a nice guy and seems like he would be a good friend. We understand each other. His wife left him and he is going through the pain of losing someone he loved, too." Martin put his head on her shoulder. She hugged him.

"Speaking of new friends," she began, "you and Diana seem to hit it off pretty well. Could it be that the days of thinking girls were covered with cooties are over?" She gave him a smile. He lifted his head.

"Very funny Mom!" She got up and walked to the doorway.

"It's getting late; you'd better hit the sack." She blew him a kiss.

"Goodnight." She turned off the light switch and began closing his door. He laid down in bed thinking about his day. He didn't think it could have gone better. He met two new friends, Mike and Diana. He was also thinking about how nice it would have been if his dad were around for him to tell of his new friends, especially of Diana.

Chapter Four

The next morning, while Martin was watching TV, there was a knock on the door. His mom answered it, and he was interrupted from his program to hear his mom say, "Diana's here to see you." He just about jumped off the couch and ran to the door. He had to stop himself from seeming too happy to see her standing there.

"So do you fish?" she asked.

"Huh?" Her question caught him off guard. She stood there in the doorway holding a fishing pole and wearing cut-off shorts and a T-shirt. He was surprised at how nice she looked dressed like that.

"I asked if you fish." she said. He smiled and scratched his head.

"Well, I haven't since I went with my dad about four years ago. Why?"

"Because, silly, I want to know if you want to go fishing with me."

"I don't have a pole." he began. She interrupted him.

"I have a spare". She picked up a pole that was leaning up by the door and waved it so he could see.

"Now are you coming are aren't ya?" Teresa yelled from the kitchen, "Be careful, lunch will be ready in an hour."

"Sure mom." He walked out the front door, closing it behind him.

"So where are we going fishing?" She smiled at him and winked.

"It's a secret." She quickly took off running.

"Wait!" He grabbed the fishing pole and ran to catch her.

"Come on!" she yelled back as she took off down a path behind the field. He ran fast to catch up with her. It was hard to run with the pole in his hand. She was moving pretty fast before him. Finally, she came to another path and stopped. When he caught up with her, he was too out of breath to ask her why she ran. She was out of breath too. She reached in her pocket and pulled out an inhaler and inhaled twice. She took deep breaths and it seemed to help. He remembered she had said she had asthma. After a moment, she spoke up.

"I don't want any of the other kids to know where we're going, especially Randy. He'll squeal to Mike." She pointed towards a set of trees.

"Behind there. That's my secret fishing hole. Now you can't tell any of the other kids that I brought you here okay?"

"Okay!" he agreed.

"Good." she said and smiled. Martin didn't understand why she didn't want Mike to know, but he didn't ask. She waved him to follow her.

"Come on." She walked up the path a few feet and sat down on the bank by a stream. He followed and sat down next to her. He looked around. He could see why she had picked that spot as her secret fishing hole. It was a great quite place to sit and be alone. He liked being alone with her. It was the second time that no one else was with them but this time he wasn't feeling nervous, trying to find something to talk about. She reached down next to her and pulled a small tin pail from the ground.

"This is where I keep my worms." She reached in and grabbed one of the worms and began putting it on the hook. Martin was surprised to see her baiting her own hook with a worm. Most of the girls he had known back in San Diego would never get anywhere near that close to a worm, much less hook it without gagging or complaining. It blew his mind how much she could do. One minute she's singing like an angel dressed up in church clothes looking lovely, the next she's in cut-off jean shorts, a T-shirt and sitting at a fishing hole hooking a worm. He had never met a girl like Diana. She noticed him looking at her as he was thinking and she spoke up.

"Do you want me to do it for you or do you think you can handle it?" she asked jokingly. He gave her a sharp look and grabbed a worm from the pail and began hooking it. She smiled at him to let him know she was kidding with him. They both put their lines in the water. As they sat there, they began to talk.

"So, what happened to your dad?" He looked down at his line for a moment before he spoke up.

"He was a pilot, an amazing one. He flew to Italy on a deployment for six months. On his way back, his plane got lost off the radar. I didn't believe it at first. I kept waiting for him to walk through the front door and give me a big hug and say

"Sorry I'm late!" But when they finally found his plane the next morning, there was no chance of that." She was sad to hear his story about his father's death. She looked down toward the water. He continued.

"Anyway, my mom decided it was too painful to stay there on base at Camp Pendleton where his memory was, so she put in for orders to move here. I guess she wanted to get as far away from that memory as possible. She decided to move clear across the country."

"I guess so." Diana said softly.

"Anyway," he continued, "I'm gonna go to Paris Island and train to be a Marine when I turn 18. I'm gonna be a pilot like my dad." He looked up and smiled at her. She smiled back. There was a moment of silence. She looked back down at her line.

"My mom is gone too. She's not dead though. She's a pretty famous singer and actress. She taught me how to sing too. One day she got an offer to move to New York to be in a Broadway play. Daddy didn't want her to go and leave him and me but she didn't want to miss her opportunity at fame and she left anyway. She's in California now. She does some movies, some little stuff. She sends me a post card and an occasional check on my birthdays." She stopped to look around. She thought she heard a noise but didn't see anyone.

"I'm going to be a singer like she is." she said.

"I'm a pretty good singer." Martin looked up at her.

"I know." He had said it before he realized what he had done. Diana perked up her head from the water she had been looking at.

"It was you that night, wasn't it?" She asked. He looked up at her and tried to hide his guilty face.

"It was you looking in the window while I was singing, wasn't it? She was becoming a little cross with him.

"It's very rude to go sneaking around spying on people you know!" she said angrily. He felt bad. He didn't want her mad at him. They sat in silence for a moment. He wanted to say he was sorry but she seemed pretty mad at him.

"Well, you're very good!" he said. She smiled.

"Thanks. My mom taught me before she left." They both just sat there with their fishing lines in the water. After a moment she looked over at him.

"Martin, will you do me a favor?" He looked at her.

"Sure, what?" She continued with her question.

"When you become a pilot, will you promise to give me a ride up in your plane?" Martin smiled at her and she smiled at him.

"Sure, I promise. But only if you promise me that when you become a famous singer and win an award, you'll remember me." She gave him a smile and held out her hand for him to shake.

"Deal?" she asked. He took her hand and shook it.

"Deal." Just then, Martin's line started to pull. He looked down at his pole.

"Whoa, I got one!" he said excitedly. She looked at his pole.

"Wow, get it before it gets away." He reached down and began reeling in the fish. He had trouble reeling it in and she helped him by pulling on the line. The fish was strong and unwilling to give in.

"Pull harder!" They both gave one strong pull and the fish came out of the water. He was a big fish, almost a foot long.

"Wow, look at him." she said.

"He's a big fellow!" They both sat for a moment looking at the fish while Martin held up the line. He was proud of himself. He thought about how his dad would have been proud of him too. Diana and Martin sat looking at the fish and each other. They both felt sorry for it flopping around. After a moment, Diana spoke up.

"He looks so sad, Martin." He nodded his head.

"Yeah,"

"We need to throw him back in now." she said.

"I don't want him to die."

"Then we'll save him. He will live another day." He worked the hook out of its mouth, and lowered the fish back into the water.

"Maybe he'll remember how we saved his life" said Diana. They both giggled. Martin thought it was strange how she wanted to go fishing, only to let it go. Oddly, it only made him like her more. After they were done fishing, they went to Diana's house to return the fishing poles. It was pretty hot outside and the air conditioning felt wonderful as they stepped inside the front door. She put down her pole in a closet by the front door and he did the same.

"Want something to drink?" she asked him.

"Oh, you bet." He followed her into the kitchen. She opened the refrigerator and took out two orange sodas. She handed him one and he thanked her. They both opened their cans and took a drink. They were silent for a moment. He looked around her living room. There was a painting of a maiden kissing a knight by a stream hanging above the couch. Their furniture looked very expensive. They had nice things. He guessed that her dad was pretty high up in rank to be able to afford all this stuff.

"So, what does your dad do?" he asked her.

"He's a Gunny Sergeant. He is head of an office on base. He deals with a lot of paperwork. Fun stuff!" she said with a chuckle.

"Oh."

"So what does your mother do?" she asked him.

"She's a nurse. She works at the hospital here on base. She's been in the Marines for about 16 years now." Diana walked over to the TV, turned it on and sat down on the couch. He followed her and sat down next to her. Diana took a drink and put her can on the coffee table. Martin did the same.

On the TV was a movie he had seen years ago with his father. There was a woman looking worried that the man she loved was going away to war. She was afraid he would be killed and that they would never see each other again. The man gave her a tender kiss and promised he would never really be away from her. Then he got on the train. It made Martin blush a little watching such a kiss while sitting next to Diana. He was thinking of something to say to change the awkward mood but she spoke up first.

"Martin, do you really believe that a man would love a woman enough that he would always love her, even being apart for so long?" He didn't know how to respond to that. He never gave the subject a thought before.

"I uh, well.. I know my mom and dad loved each other very much. I know Mom misses my Dad so much that she would give anything just to see him again. I would say they loved each other like that. I'd say yes, I believe it." It must have been the right answer because Diana smiled at him.

"Me too!" Just then, there was a knock on the door. She got up and answered it. Mike was standing there, holding a baseball in his hand.

"We're starting up a game. Do you want to play?"

"Sure," she said.

"I'll go get my glove and mask." She took off to her room. Mike noticed Martin sitting on the couch and waved at him.

"Hey, Martin. You joining the game too?" Mike asked him with a smile.

"Sure." Martin turned off the TV.

"Good." You go home and get your cap and glove and we'll meet you on the field. I need to tell Diana something real quick." Mike walked back to Diana's room and Martin left for home to get his cap and glove.

On his way to his bedroom, Martin grabbed the sandwich his mother had made for him that was sitting on the counter. His mom was in the shower getting ready for her first day of work. He found his glove and cap sitting on his dresser where he had left them from the last baseball game. He finished the sandwich quickly. On his way out of the house, he grabbed the glass of milk that had been sitting on the counter next to the sandwich and guzzled it down.

Out on the field, Martin saw the kids from the last game. He was surprised that Mike and Diana hadn't shown up yet. The kids were in three little groups talking. One kid noticed Martin approaching and waved at him. Just then, Mike and Diana showed up. It looked to Martin like they were arguing. Mike looked up and yelled, "Alright, let's get this game going. Time to pick our teams." All the kids got out of their groups and formed a half circle around Mike.

"I'll pick a team and Randy, you pick a team." said Mike.

"I pick Martin." Mike began.

"Ah man!" said Randy.

"Well, I pick Chris." A boy from the crowd shouted, "Alright!"

"Well, I pick David." said Mike. Back and forth they went picking their team players. When they were done, everyone broke off into their teams.

"I'll be designated pitcher for both teams. Randy, your team is up to bat first!" he yelled. After Mike told the teams their playing positions, they all went to their designated spots on the field. Martin was once again on third base while Mike was pitcher. Randy was the first up to bat. He grabbed a bat from the ground and made a few practice swings. Behind him a cute blond girl named Karen Sims cheered him on.

"Hey Randy, you think you could hit a home run for me?" She gave him a smile. He turned towards her.

"Girl, what's wrong with you? Can't you see I'm doing something important here?" He rolled his eyes and turned back to the game.

"Girls!" he said.

"Hey Mike, I'm gonna knock this puppy into the next county!"

"Put your money where your mouth is!" Mike yelled back. He wound up his arm and threw the ball. Randy swung and missed. The ball went sailing by him, almost hitting Diana.

"Strike!" yelled Diana.

"Darn it. I wasn't ready!" yelled Randy.

"Well get ready, cause here it comes again!" Mike yelled at Randy. Mike wound up his arm again and Randy readied his stance. Mike pitched the ball and Randy swung; this time, he hit the ball and it went towards third base. Randy took off running. Martin quickly caught the ball and threw it to first base. The kid on first caught it and Randy was out. Randy yelled a few obscenities and went to sit down where his other team members were sitting. Martin kept looking over at Diana. She seemed slightly upset. It must have been the conversation she and Mike had had in private. She looked up at Martin and they exchanged smiles. Martin's attention was drawn away as he heard a car door shut. He looked up and saw his mom putting her purse in the car. Martin called a time out and ran over to her.

"Where's he going?" asked Mike.

"It looks like he's going to tell his mom bye!" said Chris, the boy beside Randy. Randy started to laugh.

"That's so lame."

"No it's not!" shot back Diana.

"I think it's sweet." Mike looked over at Diana who was watching Martin walk over to his mother's car. Mike gave her a disappointed look. Diana glanced over at Mike, saw his look, and stopped smiling. Martin's mom saw him and smiled.

"I have to leave for work now. I'll call you later. Dinner is in the refrigerator. Just take the casserole dish out and put it in the oven on 350 for 30 minutes, okay?"

"Okay mom. Good luck." She smiled at him and was going to give him a hug but stopped herself.

"Since your friends are watching, I'll hold off on the hug till later."

"Thanks."

"If you need anything, my work number is on the fridge." She got in the car and he told her goodbye.

She shut the door, started the engine, pulled the car out and drove off. He turned and went back to the game. When he walked back to the field, Mike, who had been so nice to him so far, gave him an angry look and said

"Alright, let's play." Martin couldn't tell why Mike and Diana were acting so weird. But whatever reason it was, it was making Mike mad, Diana sad, and Martin confused. They continued their game, and when it was time for Martin to bat, he walked up to the base and whispered, "What's wrong?" to Diana.

"Nothing, just forget it," she whispered back to him.

"No, I can't." he said softly.

"Did I do something wrong?"

"No." she whispered.

"I did."

"What did you do?" They were still whispering.

"You better get ready, cause here comes the ball!" Mike yelled to Martin. Martin quickly turned around, swung the bat up onto his shoulder, and took his stance. Mike wound up his arm and threw the pitch. It hit Martin in the shoulder.

"Ouch!" he said softly, rubbing where the ball hit him.

"Oops, sorry." Mike said sarcastically. Diana gave Mike a mean look.

"Are you alright?"

"I'm fine." He winked, but turned and gave Mike a confused look.

"Foul!" she yelled. Martin took a few practice swings, put the bat back on his shoulder and got ready. He didn't know what kind of mind game Mike was playing with him, but he wasn't about to let himself get beat. Mike spit on the ball, wound up his pitch and threw the ball as hard as he could. This time, Martin was ready. He swung the bat with all his might. The bat hit the ball with such force that the bat strongly vibrated in his hand causing pain. He tossed the bat aside and while everyone's eyes were on the ball that was quickly traveling towards the woods, Martin ran a home run. The same boy, who went in the woods to retrieve the ball from the home run Martin made from the last game, headed towards the woods.

"Oh man, not again!" As Martin came sliding into home, he was greeted by his team members cheering for him. He looked back at Mike, who took off his hat and threw it down. He was sulking. Martin started walking towards Mike to see why he was so mad, but Chris grabbed his arm and stopped him in his tracks.

"Man, you really pissed him off!"

"What did I do?" Martin asked Chris.

"Randy caught you up at Diana's secret spot in the woods. Guess it's not very secret, huh?" Martin gave him a glare.

"So?"

"So", no one is supposed to go there with Diana except Mike, get it?" Martin looked surprised.

"You mean they're a couple?"

"Well, not technically, but according to Mike, they are. To Diana, he's just a friend. But that doesn't stop Mike from getting possessive of her. Why, last summer, I heard he punched some poor kid's nose just because the kid opened a door for her at the movies."

"Oh, really?"

"Yep. So if I were you, I'd leave Diana alone."   Chris walked away too early to hear Martin say, "Not a chance!" Just then, it started raining. Everyone ran off to their homes, yelling goodbye to each other. Martin and Diana just stood looking at each other. Mike was still standing on the pitcher's mound looking at Diana. Seeing his face, she looked down. For a moment, the three of them stood in the rain. Mike looked from Diana to Martin and then walked away as if giving in to defeat. Diana watched Mike waking away. She looked at Martin, then down to the ground, and then walked away, leaving Martin alone on the field confused.

Chapter Five

Martin had just made it to his bedroom when he heard a knocking on the front door. He went to answer it, and seeing who it was, he gave Diana a little smile and asked her if she wanted to come in.

"Thanks!" she said. After she had stepped in and Martin closed the front door behind her, they both just stood there. He didn't know what to say. She seemed to be deep in thought.

"Mike is a nice guy, Martin." she said.

"You just don't understand him yet." she explained. She had her hands shoved in her short pockets, warming up her hands that had gotten a bit chilly from the rain. She looked down at the floor for a few seconds.

"He seems to have gotten it in his head that somewhere along the way my friendship to him had become something more. I have told him over and over how I'm just his friend. He just has trouble accepting it, I guess." Martin kept his eyes on her, listening to her every word. She continued.

"I saw Chris talking to you. Did he tell you to be careful around Mike and to leave me alone?"

"Yep!"

"And did he tell you that Mike once punched some kid's nose just for opening a door for me?" Martin smiled and nodded.

"Well, that wasn't true at all. The door accidentally hit the kid's nose as he opened it for me, and Mike just told him to be careful. Mike is a really nice guy. That's the way it really happened. Chris can really exaggerate sometimes." She leaned back against the door waiting for him to say something. When he didn't, she spoke up.

"When me and Mike were talking in private earlier, he wanted to know how I could bring someone else to my secret place. I told him we were just friends and it wasn't his business. That got him mad at me and I guess he was jealous of you." The thought of Mike being jealous of him made Martin give a little smile. She continued, "Anyway, I just wanted to let you know why Mike seemed weird earlier." She waited for him to say something, but when he didn't, she turned to leave.

"Well, I guess I'll see you around."

"Wait!" He put his hand on her shoulder and turned her around.

"Do you want to play a game or something?"

"Sure, like what?" she asked. He thought for a moment.

"How about checkers?"

"Sure, that sounds fun."

"I have it in my closet. Come on." He led her to his room. When they got there, he picked up a few shirts that were on the floor and tossed them into his laundry basket. She took a look around his room. His walls had posters with aircraft on them. Hanging down from a hook was a scene of the solar system. His room was the same size as hers. In fact, the houses were the same, just reversed. He walked over to his closet and went through the game boxes he had up on the closet shelf. She looked out his window and saw it faced her bedroom window.

"Hey, our windows face each other," she said.

"We could send each other messages or something."

"Yeah!" he said as he grabbed the checkers game and pulled it out of the closet. She turned around to see him standing behind her holding the game.

"We can play here on the floor or the kitchen table if you like." he told her.

"Here is fine. More comfortable I think."

"Me too." he said with a smile. They both squatted down and they laid out the game. As they were getting the game ready, she asked him a question.

"Do you have a best friend?"

"No, how about you?"

"No, most kids I know are boys, and they don't want a girl as their best friend. Especially one with asthma who's not supposed to run." She looked down at the red game piece she was holding and moved it around in her fingers as she thought for a moment.

"We can be best friends, if you want." she finally said. He looked at her with a smile.

"Sure!"

"That is, if you don't mind a girl as a best friend." He smiled, almost blushing.

"Nope! I don't mind at all." He was trying to hide his excitement of being her best friend. Who knows where that might lead to one day?

"Hey Martin, do you think you'll ever get married someday?" That question caught him by surprise. It wasn't something he was expecting her to ask at that moment. He thought it was funny how she caught him off guard with some of her questions. That's one of the things he found interesting about her.

"I think so, why?" he said with a shrug.

"Well, if we're best friends now, then maybe when we each get married, our kids will be best friends too." She smiled.

"Maybe." he said with a little smile.

"But we both have plenty of time before we have kids of our own someday." They played checkers three times and each time, she beat him. When it had gotten suppertime, they said their good-byes and she went home. As he stood in the doorway watching her walk home, he thought about how lucky he was to have her as his best friend, and how he was hers. He couldn't help feeling that he wanted more. He wanted her to be his girlfriend, but he knew she only wanted to be his friend, like with Mike. He could understand how Mike wanted more. He liked Mike.

Mike was the first kid to welcome him to Beaufort. He wondered if Diana had ever asked Mike to be her best friend. He closed the front door and went to warm up his dinner in the oven. He didn't like eating alone, but he was used to it. Since his dad died, his mom had been working nights back in California and he was alone on evenings, but he never really got used to it. After finishing his dinner, Martin watched TV. His favorite show was on, but he wasn't paying much attention to it. He was too busy thinking about Diana, wondering if she was thinking about him. He was enjoying his summer, more than he thought he would, thanks to her.

The weeks following were filled with ball games, trips to the secret fishing hole with Diana, and when all the kids finished building a tree house in the woods, they had secret meetings there. Their meetings really consisted of eating snacks, talking about how much they hated summer to end and playing cards. Martin and Diana grew close that summer and so did he and Mike. They became like brothers. Martin noticed how Mike spent less and less time at home, and more time up in the tree house. Martin knew things weren't great for him at home. His dad and he didn't get along, and his mother was hardly at home.

Martin spent as much time as he could with Mike to take his mind off his troubled home life. Before Martin knew it, the summer was almost over. He had adapted very well to his new home. Two weeks before school was about to start, Mike invited Martin and Diana to go walking in the woods up a path he had found.

"It leads up to a cliff where you can see clear across the river." he explained to them. Martin and Diana thought it sounded exciting, so they agreed to go. They followed Mike while he led the way. As they were walking, Mike was telling them how he had found the cliff. He had been walking one night after his dad came home drunk and started yelling at him and his mother. He had left to be by himself and just kept walking. He ended up by the cliff and climbed up on it and just sat there, looking across the water. He told them it was the most beautiful place he had ever seen.

"So peaceful and quiet." They walked for what seemed like a mile in the woods when finally, Mike stopped and pointed to a slope of rocks to their left that was about 20 feet high.

"This is it!" he said.

"Just climb up these rocks and you will get there." Martin and Diana looked up at the big wall of rocks and neither one of them felt very sure about climbing up there.

"I don't know," said Diana.

"It doesn't look too safe."

"Yeah, Mike, I mean one slip, and you could really get hurt." said Martin. Mike rolled his eyes at them.

"Ah, come on you two. It's easy; just climb up the rocks like stairs. Here, I'll show you." Mike jumped onto the lowest rock and started climbing up. His foot slipped a few times but he made it up to the top. When he got there, he stood up and yelled down to them.

"You see? It's easy. You just have to get your balance and start climbing." Mike looked up and around him.

"The view up here is incredible." he called down to them.

"You should see it." Diana looked at Martin.

"Well, here goes!" She put her left foot up on the first small rock and pulled herself up. Martin got behind her and started climbing, keeping his eyes on her. He wanted to be as close to her as possible so he could catch her if she slipped. Martin realized that climbing the rocks wasn't as hard as he thought. Before they knew it, Diana and Martin were almost at the top. Mike reached down and gave them both a hand. Then they were at the top looking around. Mike was right, thought Martin.

The view was incredible. They had to be a good 30 feet up from the river bank down below. He could see far from up there. Off in the distance to the right, he could see rooftops of the houses they lived in. Mike sat down and Martin and Diana sat down too. For a moment, they sat quietly. Then Mike began to talk.

"School's, about to start soon, and our summer fun will be over." He sighed and continued.

"Mom said she and my dad are getting a divorce." Diana and Martin looked at each other puzzled and looked back at Mike.

"That means that this may be my last summer here. She wants this divorce as soon as possible and wants to move away from Dad. He does nothing but drink when he's at home, and yells at us like a drill instructor. I think he's been hitting her too." He gave a small giggle with a half smile.

"Funny how you can be one way one moment, then have a few drinks and turn into a monster the next. He doesn't deserve Mom." Mike paused for a moment; his expression changed to a more serious one.

"Man, I don't want to grow up. I don't want to be anything like him. I don't want to end up treating my wife like that." Mike's expression was grim.

"Mike, you're nothing like him." said Diana

"Yeah, Mike. You don't have to be like your dad." added Martin.

"You don't have to make the same bad choices. You'll see. It'll be fine!" Mike and Martin exchanged glances at Diana.

"Yeah, right," was Mike's response. All of a sudden, Mike stood up. He began to yell orders like a drill instructor.

"Alright Marines, on your feet!" Martin and Diana looked up at Mike, then at each other, smiled and stood at attention like soldiers.

"You Marines are pathetic." Mike continued.

"Your clothes are wrinkled. You're a disgrace to your uniform." Both Martin and Diana tried to keep a straight face but couldn't help but laugh.

"Do you think this is a game? Don't smile when I'm speaking." Mike's voice got louder and more threatening. Martin and Diana's smiles faded. Mike continued his drill.

"You're pathetic, you're nothing. You'll never amount to anything. Do you hear me? You can't do anything right. You're worthless." Martin and Diana looked at each other confused. Mike's game was more than just a game now. He was no longer acting like Mike. He was acting like his father. Martin put his hand on Mike's shoulder.

"Hey man, I know he's tough on you. He's wrong to be like that. But you could never be like him. You're too good for that." Mike looked down at Martin and Diana, then down to the ground for a moment deep in thought.

"Mike, you're a great person and friend. Don't forget that!" Diana said. After a moment of silence, Mike picked up a rock. His voice was back to normal.

"Hey Martin, the one who throws a rock the farthest gets.." He thought for a moment.

"Gets a kiss from Diana." Diana giggled. Mike got close to the edge and threw his rock. It made it into the water below but not far. Martin liked that challenge and he reached down and grabbed rocks. They both started throwing rocks to see who could get their rock the farthest. Mike was so busy trying to win that he didn't notice just how close to the edge his feet were. He picked up another rock and threw it, but just as he did, his foot slipped and he began to fall.

"Mike!" Diana screamed. Martin quickly grabbed hold of Mike's arm just in time to catch him. Martin fell to the ground on his stomach still holding onto Mike's arm with all his might. Mike dangled over the edge while Martin held on tight. Martin reached down with his other arm and grabbed Mike's arm. Diana reached down and grabbed Mike's arm with both her hands. Mike's face was filled with terror.

"Please, man, don't let go!" he pleaded with Martin.

"I won't. Not a chance." assured Martin.

"Don't look down. Just look at me." Mike tried to get a foothold on the side of the cliff but couldn't find one. His feet kept sliding.

"Come on, Mike. Climb up!" Diana was crying.

"I can't!" Mike cried out.

"You have to try." explained Martin.

"Come on, Mike. Try!" Mike found a foothold and began lifting himself up. But just as he put pressure on the rock, it broke off and he slipped even further down. Martin and Diana grabbed even tighter onto Mike's arm.

"You have to go get help, Diana." Martin yelled at her.

"Hurry!" She took off down the rock wall as fast as she could with care, and when she got down to the ground, she ran. Martin was losing strength trying to hold onto Mike. Suddenly, Mike began slipping even further down.

"Oh God, Don't let me fall!" he pleaded out. Martin's fingers were white from holding onto Mike's arm so tightly. Mike slipped down to where Martin could only hold onto his hand. Martin and

Mike looked at each other eye to eye up until Mike's hand slid down to Martin's fingers.

"Hang on Mike, she's going to get help!" Mike kept his eyes on Martin.

"You know Mike," Martin said.

"I think your rock went farther. I think you won, buddy. So just hold on!"

"I can't." Said Mike in a shaky voice. After a moment, Mike softly said

"Hey Martin, She got to me too...But you see, it didn't matter how hard I threw. She already chose.... It's okay though..... She chose right." Just then Mike's hand slid down further and Martin lost his grip.

"NO!" Martin screamed out as he watched his friend fall 30 feet to the rocks below. Diana, who hadn't made it out of the woods yet, heard Martin's scream. Knowing what had happened, she fell to the ground crying.

Martin and Diana stood with Teresa in the waiting area of the emergency room as Mike's parents were talking with the doctor. Martin held Diana's hand as they were listening to the doctor explain Mike's condition.

"He fell down a cliff and hit his head on a rock. He was knocked unconscious and we can't wake him." Mike's mom spoke up.

"What does that mean?"

"It means that he is in a coma and we don't know when or if he will wake up." the doctor explained.

Mike's mom began sobbing while her husband stood by showing little emotion.

"If? What do you mean if?" His dad finally spoke up.

"That's my boy! Of course he is going to wake up. He's strong! I taught him to fight, be strong and…" Mike's mom interrupted him…"You taught him how not to be by coming home drunk and yelling at us. He saw how you were and didn't want to be like that! He's so much better than that! Why can't you see how good he is? If for once you would have put down the bottle, sobered up and paid him attention then maybe this wouldn't have happened."

"Don't you dare blame this on me!" Mikes dad yelled at her as he pointed his finger. The doctor quickly interrupted at that moment.

"He needs you to stay strong and pull together for him, not fight. You won't do him any good acting like this! What he needs to hear right now is your loving voices. He needs to know you are there for him." Both were quiet after he spoke and they looked at each other.

"He's right." She said.

"This isn't a time to argue. Please, I would like to see my son now." Her husband interrupted.

"Our son." The doctor spoke up.

"OK. You may go in and see him now but please, show him only your love." He led Mike's parents to the room where Mike was. Martin and Diana had to wait in the waiting room with Martin's mom. Diana began to cry.

"He's just got to be okay. He's just got to." Martin put his arm around her to comfort her.

"Mike is strong! He's the toughest guy I've ever met." After about 10 minutes, Martin and Diana saw

Mike's parents walk out of Mike's room and walk past them.

"He looks so peaceful." Mike's mom said between sobs as her husband led her away.

"I wish they would allow us to go see him." said Diana. Teresa looked down at Diana and Martin.

"Well, I'll make them bend the rules for me this one time. Come on." she said and led them to Mike's room. As they rounded the corner to Mike's room, Teresa looked around and saw that no one was looking. She quickly hurried them into his doorway. Inside, Mike was hooked up to several machines. Some were beeping. Tubes and wires were sticking out of his arms and chest. His face was covered with bruises and scrapes. Martin hardly recognized him. They walked slowly over to his bed and looked down at his face. He did look peaceful, even under all the bruises and wires. They just stood there for a few moments. They didn't know what to say. Diana slowly reached down and held Mike's hand.

"Mike, it's me, Diana." she said as she wiped a tear away with her other hand.

"Squeeze my hand if you hear." Mike made no movement. Tears were flowing down her cheek. She looked at Martin with a helpless expression. He spoke up.

"Mike, I'm here too. You're gonna be alright. In a few days, you'll be throwing me fast pitches and you'll strike me out. Wait and see." Martin made a half smile to Mike. He continued.

"Mike, you were the first friend I made when I moved here. I know you're going to get better." Just then, a nurse came into the room and whispered something to Teresa. Teresa walked up beside Martin.

"It's time for us to go now." Diana softly said

"Bye, Mike." and she bent down and gave Mike a kiss on the cheek. After she walked away, Martin bent down and whispered in Mike's ear.

"See, you did win Mike, because you got the kiss." Martin stood there for a moment; waiting for a sign from Mike. As he finally started to turn away to leave, he saw a weak smile form on Mike's lips, or maybe he just imagined it.

"Bye, Mike," said Martin. They left the room, never taking their eyes off Mike. Teresa drove Martin and Diana home. Neither one of them said much in the car. Diana stopped and bought them all ice cream, which neither ate much of. When the car finally pulled up to Martin's house, Diana's dad was waiting on the lawn. He had a grim expression on his face. Diana got out of the parked car and went over to him and asked him what was wrong. James paused for a moment before finally speaking up.

"Mike's dad just called from the hospital," James explained.

"Mike had internal bleeding. The doctors did all they could for him. They just couldn't do any more." He looked down at Diana and put his hands on her shoulders.

"He's gone, Diana." he said to her. He tried putting his arm around her shoulder to comfort her. She just stood there a moment, not really understanding what was going on. She couldn't be hearing him right. After a moment, she pushed him away.

"No, he can't be!" she screamed.

"No, you're lying! He's fine, he's just fine!" She took off running.

"Come back, Diana!" her dad yelled to her, but she kept running. Martin spoke up.

"I know where she's going. I'll be back." Martin ran off after her. She ran towards the woods behind their houses, then down the path. He knew right where she was heading. Martin could no longer see her as she disappeared behind a group of trees. He stopped and caught his breath. Then he heard her sobbing. He followed the sound and it led him to where she was sitting. He sat down beside her and put his arm around her. She tried pushing him away, but he held on tighter. She gave in and leaned in, putting her head on his shoulder. He just sat there holding her as she cried.

"He can't be gone." she said as she sobbed.

"He was my friend."

"I know, he was my friend too." he said to her, "and I'm gonna miss him too!" She sat up and wiped the tears away from her cheeks and eyes. She stopped crying and sat silent for a moment. Finally, she spoke up.

"He helped me pass 4th grade. When my mom left I was doing poorly in math and he came over every day for a month just to help me get my grade up. I probably wouldn't have passed if he hadn't done that for me." She looked up at Martin. He could see by the look in her eyes that Mike meant a lot to her.

"That was a nice thing that he did for you."

"Yes, it was." she said. She gave him a smile. For a moment they sat in silence, looking at each other. He wanted so badly to lean in and kiss her. She was so lovely. If only she felt more for him than she did, then maybe he could kiss her. But she didn't and he didn't want to spoil the friendship they had. She trusted him and needed him there for her. He saw it in her eyes. He was almost sure she was going to lean in and kiss him, when finally she spoke up.

"Martin, will you stay and sit here with me for a while?" He was thrilled that she wanted him there with her.

"Sure. As long as you wish" he answered.

"Until I forget." she said. She leaned over and rested her head on his shoulder. He reached over and held her hand. They both just sat there in silence until the sun went down. It was a closed casket ceremony. It was too painful for Mike's mom to see him. Martin was grateful for that decision too. It was hard enough seeing his friend lying in the hospital bed. He knew Diana didn't need to see him that way either. The chaplain gave a service about moving on into the gates of heaven and having eternal life. About how you don't die, but are reborn in God's kingdom. Diana was asked by Mike's mom to sing a song at the service. She didn't want to at first. She was too sad. But Martin talked her into it.

"I'm sure he would want you to sing, Diana." he had told her.

"I know I would." She reluctantly agreed. She sounded lovely, as her father played piano while she stood at the front of the chapel and sang a slow hymn. Martin couldn't take his eyes off her. Even while in grief, she was the most beautiful person to him. She warmed his heart with her song. He had to wipe tears away from his eyes as she sang. After the ceremony, everyone headed to the cemetery to watch Mike's burial. Martin was reminded of how awful it was to see his dad's casket being lowered in the ground at his funeral. He wanted to get out of the cemetery fast. He looked up off into the distance and his mind went back to that day. Martin didn't want to go that morning. He never wanted to go anywhere again. He just wanted to sit in his room.

Looking down at his father in the casket was heart-wrenching. No more baseball games where his dad would be cheering him on from the bleachers. No more father/son fishing trips where they would stay out late, drink way too much soda and tell each other the latest jokes. No more trips to the air show to see his dad fly. No more of life as he knew it, as he needed it to be.

Martin was brought back to the present by sobs from Mike's mom. He looked over at her and was surprised to see her husband standing there with his hand on her shoulder, comforting her as he wiped away a tear from his eye. For a moment Martin thought that maybe this whole death was Mike's plan to get them together again. He imagined that Mike was probably looking down from Heaven smiling at his handy work. Martin looked over at Diana to see how she was doing. She just kept her eyes down. Martin didn't know what to say to her but he wanted to give her time to grieve. He reached over and held her hand. She looked over at him to acknowledge him and looked back down.

The reception was at Mike's parent's house. The house was filled with food and people who came to pay their respects. The kids from the neighborhood were there. Mostly though, it was Mike's relatives; people Martin and Diana had never met before. Teresa and James were talking with the other parents about how awful this all must be on Mike's parents. Diana and Martin went out and sat on the back porch. They didn't really want to be around those people. Diana hadn't really talked much since the day of the accident. Martin thought, maybe she is trying to sort things out in her head, to make sense of it all. That's the way Martin was after he lost his dad. It just wasn't fair, Martin thought, how life took away the people you cared about without warning, and without reason. Diana just sat there on the porch swing, looking down.

"Do you want something to eat?" Martin asked her.

"No, thanks."

"Do you want to go for a walk or something?"

"No, I don't feel like it."   She turned to him.

"Martin? Why did this happen? Why do things like this happen? Why do the people you care about suddenly get taken away from you? It's not fair!" Tears were welling up in her eyes. He wanted to stop her, to say something but he knew she needed to let it out.

"Dad keeps telling me that Mike's in a better place, but how can he say that? Mike was just a kid. He played baseball, he went to school and liked to play video games and eat pizza. He was too young, Martin. Why would God take him now? He was supposed to grow up and play professional baseball. That was his dream! I don't understand! I don't understand why we are sitting here and he isn't. I don't understand why we can get up, go to school, eat a pizza or even play baseball again in that crummy field when he can't." She was sobbing now. Finally he spoke up.

"I don't know. I don't know why he's gone. I don't know why these things happen, why you can be talking, laughing with someone one moment, and then suddenly they're gone. But what I do know is somehow, someway we go on. One day you smile without realizing. You laugh at a joke; you sing along to a song on the radio and realize that life still goes on for you. I don't know much about these things, but what I've found out is that somehow, someway we go on. I guess we realize that we have to live for them, so they can live on through us I guess." For a moment they both sat in silence. Her sobs stopped and as she wiped away her tears, she looked back at him.

"Martin?"

"Yes?"

"Thanks." He smiled.

"Anytime!" He suddenly got an idea to make her laugh.

"So, you wanna go skinny dipping?" he asked her with a smile. She looked up, and with a slight giggle asked

"What?"

"Ah, I got you to smile." She then realized she had smiled; something she hadn't been able to do for days.

"Thanks for trying to cheer me up."

"No problem, that's what best friends are for." he said. She gave him another smile. Martin pointed to her mouth.

"See, there it is again. Her smile lives on." Later that night, Martin was lying in bed thinking when he heard a tap on his bedroom window. He got up and looked out. Diana was standing outside his window.

"You can't sleep either?" he asked.

"No. I keep thinking about Mike."

"Yeah, me too. Come with me!" Martin crawled out the window and they headed to the trampoline in the back yard of Diana's house. They laid down and for a few moments, they just looked up at the night sky in silence. Then Diana spoke up.

"Martin?"

"Yeah?"

"Do you think it maybe wasn't an accident?"

"What do you mean?" He asked. She paused for a moment.

"I mean, what if he wanted out?" Martin thought for a second.

"I know things were rough for him at home. But I guess we'll never really know what was in his head."

"Yeah, I guess not." There was a moment of silence.

"Do you think he's in heaven?"

"Definitely! I bet him and my dad are playing a game of baseball together."

"Yeah, and Mike is trying to strike him out with his fast ball!" she said with a smile. They both laughed.

"Yeah, I bet." Martin said.

"Martin?" Yeah?" He turned his head towards her.

"Thank you!"

"For what?"

"For moving here." She smiled. They looked at each other, then back up to the sky. He whispered.

"Thank you for being here!"

Chapter Six

The first day of school came quick for Martin. He didn't want the summer to be over. Starting off at a new school wasn't something he was looking forward to. Diana had promised to walk with him to school and show him around. She came by about 7:20 am when he had just finished his breakfast. He grabbed his backpack, kissed his mom goodbye, and headed out the door as his mom yelled, "Have a nice day." to him.

"I'll try." he yelled back and he and Diana headed out the door. The walk took about ten minutes. When they arrived at the school, different groups of kids were standing out in huddles around the outside. Martin and Diana walked up the stairs, past some couple holding hands and some boys bouncing a ball against the outside wall of the school. Your typical High School. She led Martin into the school and up to the office. They entered the office and the receptionist at the desk looked up and said, "Hi, Diana, welcome back to school."

"Thanks!" she said.

"This is Martin Davis and he's new here." she told the receptionist.

"Hi, Martin. I'm Mrs. Stevens and I'll get you all situated. Let's see," she said as she fingered through a stack of students' schedules.

"Davis, Martin. Here you are." She pulled out his schedule and handed it to him.

"Thanks." He took it from her.

"Diana, here's your schedule." She handed Diana hers and she and Martin left the office. She took his schedule and hers and put them together.

"Great! We have four classes together." she said.

"Cool!" he said trying to hide his enthusiasm. He had been hoping that they had at least one class together, and they had four. What luck!

"We don't have first period together, but I'll show you where you go. You have Mr. Henson as your math teacher. That's near where my first class is. You have a map of the hallways on the back of your schedule, but it's hard to read. Just follow me." She led him down the hall, past the cafeteria, past the gym, and down a smaller hallway. It seemed like they walked forever until she stopped at a door.

"This is Mr. Henson's class. I'm three doors down in Mrs. Rice's class. The bell is going to ring in a few minutes, so we better get to our classes."

"Okay, I'll see ya after class.", he said to her. She waved and walked away. She turned back around.

"Good luck!" He took a deep breath and walked into his classroom. Inside, kids were talking and laughing, huddled up into little groups. The teacher hadn't yet made it into the classroom. Up at the black board, an attractive dark-haired girl was writing

"Janet and Bobby forever". She looked over and stopped writing when she saw Martin standing there. She looked him over and gave a sly smile. She made him feel a little uneasy. I guess Bobby wasn't in this class to see the look she gave, Martin thought to himself. He returned her smile and she went to her seat, keeping her eyes on him. He found an empty desk and went to sit down. Some of the kids were looking at him because he was new, but most of the other kids weren't paying him any attention. They were too wrapped up in their gossiping to notice him.

Just then, the teacher walked in and the room grew silent. Mr. Henson was a tall, skinny man with little hair on his head. He walked over to his desk, put his briefcase down, and took his seat. I'm Mr. Henson. Welcome to my math class. I'm sure you will enjoy it as much as I will enjoy teaching it." It was more sarcasm than an honest statement. He stood up and picked up the eraser and erased the girl's message.

"I'm sure Bobby won't mind if I erase this, Janet, do you?" he asked her. Her friends giggled at her.

"No, Mr. Henson, I don't think he'll mind." she said with a silly grin as she chewed her gum and twirled her hair.

"Good, then we can begin. But before I do, I want us to pay our respects to our fellow student Mike Connor, who passed on this summer, with a moment of silence. May his soul rest in peace." The kids grew silent and lowered their heads. After the moment of silence was over, Mr. Henson gave out the textbooks and told the students to turn to page ten. He gave his lesson and before Martin knew it, the class was over. He had homework and a quiz the next day. Diana was waiting for him outside the classroom. He smiled when he saw her.

"How was your class?" she asked.

"Pretty good. I got homework already, though."

"Oh, I know, me too." she said. They had second period together, so they walked side by side to their class. It was History. Martin liked History. They sat next to each other. When lunchtime came, they went outside and sat under a tree. As they took out their sandwiches, Diana asked him, "So, what do you think of this wonderful school?" He smiled and just as he was going to answer her, Janet walked up to them. She smiled down at Martin and gave Diana a quick look of acknowledgment, and looked back at Martin and smiled even bigger.

"Hi, Martin," Janet said.

"How do you like our school so far?" Diana gave Martin a sharp look and rolled her eyes.

"So far so good." he answered.

"Diana's been showing me around and giving me advice on who to avoid, and stuff like that." Janet was twirling her hair with her finger as he spoke.

"Well, don't let Diana keep you all to herself for too long, you might miss out on something fun." Janet shot Diana a mean look and Diana returned it.

"Janet, where's Bobby? I thought you had him on a short leash these days. Aw, did he run for his life again?" Diana asked Janet sarcastically. Janet looked at Diana and squinted her eyes.

"Bobby and I have an understanding. I do whatever I want and he understands."

"Gee, Janet, sounds like the perfect loving relationship. Now if you will excuse us, we we're trying to keep our lunch down." Janet kept her eyes on Martin.

"Well, I better run. If you need anything, Martin, I'll be around." Diana looked over at Martin and saw he was still watching Janet walk away.

"Thanks for the warning!" Diana shot back. She then turned to Martin.

"Do you want to come over after school and work on our history homework together?" she asked. He didn't answer; he was still watching Janet.

"Hello, earth to Martin." Diana said.

"What?" Martin broke his stare off Janet and looked at Diana who was giving him a sarcastic look.

"What?" he asked again.

"You're staring at Janet Wilson, the girl who changes boyfriends like underwear. She's someone you'll want to avoid." Diana warned.

"She seems pretty nice to me." Martin said jokingly.

"Well, she's fake. Just try to avoid her." Martin wasn't sure, but he had thought maybe that was jealousy in Diana's voice. He grinned. When classes were over, Diana and Martin started walking home together. Chris joined them.

"Diana, did you see what Mr. Henson was wearing today? Boy what a nerd." said Chris.

"I don't know, he seems pretty cool to me." said Martin.

"You're kidding right?" asked Chris.

"I am so glad this day is over. I hate the first day of school. They always give you homework. They never cut you a break." Diana said.

"I know what you mean." said Martin.

"I didn't expect so much homework," he said as he held up his backpack. As they rounded the corner to their neighborhood street, Chris asked, "Hey, the guys and I were thinking about starting up a game today. You two want to join in?" Diana and Martin looked at each other. There hadn't been a game since Mike died. Somehow the thought of having a game without him seemed unappealing. Martin spoke up.

"We're going to do our history homework. Sorry."

"Yeah, maybe some other time." Diana added.

"Well then, okay. See ya." Chris said as he took off running to the field.

"Bye!" Martin and Diana yelled out to him. They watched him disappear past their houses to where they had played baseball with Mike. School was going good for Martin. He was getting A's and B's, thanks to his and Diana's study dates. He made new friends in his classes, and he joined the science and math clubs. He even joined the glee club, even though he could barely hold a tune, just to be with Diana. She tried out for Cheerleader and made it. That prompted Martin to try out for the football team. Diana was excited when he told her.

"Really? That's great!" she said with delight.

"If you make it, then we can ride together in the bus to the games." He wasn't too thrilled about tryouts. Football wasn't his game, but if it meant that he got to spend more time with Diana, then he was willing to go for it. When he showed up after school on the football field with the other kids trying out, he felt a little out of place. He had played football before. He and his dad played a few times when

Martin was younger, and he was on a team a few years. But it had been a while and Martin was a little rusty. Baseball was really his game. The cheerleaders were standing not too far from the field practicing. Martin glanced over at them and saw Diana waving at him. She gave him a smile and mouthed, "Good luck." He smiled when he saw her and mouthed, "Thanks." Martin wasn't paying attention as Coach Morris was calling his name.

"Martin Davis, you're up." Martin turned when he heard his name called.

"Yes?" he asked.

"I said you're up next, let's go!" Martin put on his helmet and ran on the field to his position. He stood in back and squatted down.

"Twenty-four, sixty-seven, hut! one of the players called out." He stood up and the ball was thrown his way. It took him by surprise but he caught it and ran as fast as he could. Two big guys ran towards him and tried to block him. He almost fell, but he caught is balance and slid right between them. He remembered Diana was watching, so he ran as hard and fast as he could. He was a pretty fast runner from playing baseball. The kids were running up fast behind him and he ran even harder.

The ball began to slip out of his hands. He was 50 feet away from the end zone. Diana was watching and whispering to herself, "Run Martin, run!" not paying attention to the cheerleaders beside her practicing. He tried to get a better hold on the ball, but it slipped up out of his fingers. He reached up and grabbed the ball with one hand. Just then, four guys came from behind him and jumped on him, knocking him into the end zone. Then three other kids came up and dog-piled on top of him. Diana closed her eyes to stop herself from seeing her best friend get squashed by the mound of guys.

For a moment, all was silent. Martin was completely hidden under the mound of players. Just as Diana was beginning to think he was dead, his arm popped up between two player's shoulders, holding the ball. He had made a touchdown. Diana began jumping up and down shaking her pom poms yelling, "Yeah, Martin! All right! You did it!" Her fellow cheerleaders were looking at her like she was crazy. The dog pile on Martin dissipated as players got off and stood up. Martin stood up, still holding up the ball, and smiled when he heard Diana cheering for him. The coach walked up to him and patted him on the back.

"Well, kid, congratulations. You made it. I'll see you tomorrow for practice."

"Yesss!" Martin whispered to himself. He was proud of himself. He looked over at Diana and she gave him thumbs up. He smiled. Janet had been watching from the bleachers, where she had been sitting with a group of her friends. Diana was starting to run towards Martin but Janet cut her off and ran over to Martin first.

"You made it!" Janet yelled to him, smiling and laughing. She put her arms around him, kissing his cheek. He looked at her and said, "Thanks." He looked back at Diana. She had been smiling at him but when she saw Janet run to Martin and put her arms around him, her grin faded. She didn't like seeing Martin with Janet. For some reason, it upset her. Martin saw the look on Diana's face and gently pushed Janet away.

"I better get back over with the team." he said, and ran to meet them where they were huddled. Martin looked back at Diana, as he stood in a huddle with the other players. The coach was calling out the names of the other ones who'd made the team. Diana was no longer looking at him. He sensed something in her look when Janet was hugging him. Was it jealousy he wondered, or was it something else? He was hoping for jealousy. That would mean she had feelings for him. He wanted that desperately. But he was just her friend, according to her.

The next day, Diana was acting strange. She hardly said a word to Martin as they walked to school. In class, when he leaned over from his desk and whispered to her, "What's wrong?" without even looking up from her workbook, she said

"Nothing. I'm fine!" and she began reading her lesson. He looked up at the teacher Mrs. Benson, who was busy writing their homework lesson on the board, and leaned over to Diana.

"I didn't know that Janet was going to come up and kiss me. I couldn't help it." She stopped reading, looked at him and whispered.

"Yeah, well it sure looked like you were enjoying it to me." Martin was getting mad at her behavior. He wanted to grab her by the shoulders, swing her around and say, "I'm crazy about you, stupid, not her." But instead he whispered, "Why are you acting like this? And why do you care? We're just friend, right?" Martin knew that wasn't the right thing to say, but it was too late. He had already said it. She shot him a look.

"Trying out for football just to impress a girl is stupid!" She said. He thought for a moment that she had figured him out but she continued.

"Trying to get Janet to notice you isn't worth injury out on the field. I can't believe you would stoop that low for her." He was seeing now why she was mad. She was confused. She thought it was all for Janet. She was way off. She had no idea it was for her.

"You think I did this for Janet? Diana, I did this for….."

"Silence!" Mrs. Benson interrupted.

"Whoever is talking will get detention if I am interrupted again!" Martin quickly looked down at his book so he wouldn't get caught. He tried to read. He couldn't really pay attention to his lesson. He was too upset, so he pretended to read. For days Diana acted strange around him. When she came over to study, she seemed a little withdrawn, like she had too much on her mind and no way to sort it all out. Not knowing if she was upset about Janet or if she was still thinking about Mike, Martin wasn't sure so he just gave her space. She was still being his friend and so he wasn't complaining too much. Sometimes he would catch her just staring at him and when he turned to look at her, she would quickly turn away. He wished she would talk to him about what was on her mind, but when he would ask her to, she would say,

"I'm fine," and change the subject. Diana and Martin sat in History class as the principal came on over the intercom.

"Attention students and teachers. As you know, our first game is next Friday. Following the game is our Sadie Hawkins Dance. Tickets will be on sale in the gym that morning. Please be on your best behavior while at the dance. Teacher chaperons will be attending to make sure you do so. That will be all." Martin wanted Diana to ask him to the dance. He knew she may have some feelings for him by the way she was acting jealous lately. He was looking forward to going to the dance with her, putting his arm around her during a slow dance. He figured she was just waiting for the right time to ask him. He was going to give her every opportunity after school when they walked home.

After school that day, however, Diana didn't meet Martin to walk home with. When he went to look for her, she was standing by Bobby's locker, talking with him. They were laughing and standing close to each other. Martin thought about going over there and butting in on their conversation but decided against it. Why was she talking and laughing with Janet's boyfriend? He didn't like seeing them standing so closely. He turned and walked away. He decided he wasn't going to wait for her and he began walking home alone. It hurt him seeing them together. He guessed it made him feel the way Diana must have felt seeing Janet hug and kiss him. He was brave enough to try out for football for her, but too scared to tell her how he felt, how much he cared for her. He had to tell her or he was going to go nuts. He just needed to come out and tell her. He had made his mind up. Suddenly, he was interrupted from his thoughts by her voice.

"Martin, wait!" she yelled to him. He stopped walking, and turned around to see her running towards him.

"I want to tell you something." she said as she approached him. She was wheezing a little, and had to catch her breath.

"There's something I want to tell you too." He said.

"Wait, let me go first." she began. Janet and Bobby broke up today, and I asked Bobby to the Sadie Hawkins Dance and he said yes, can you believe it?" Martin's expression turned grim. His heart seemed to stop. She had just stabbed him in the heart with a knife and was turning the blade. He couldn't tell her how he felt now.

"Sure, that's great." he said with forced enthusiasm.

"I didn't know you liked him."

"Well, neither did I until we started talking. He's really sweet, and Janet doesn't deserve him." Diana saw that Martin was frowning.

"Hey, if Janet asks you, we could all go together." Martin was looking down at the ground.

"Sure, Okay." he said softly.

"Great!" She smiled.

"I've got to go. We have cheerleading practice. I just wanted you to be the first to know. She turned to leave but stopped.

"What was it you wanted to tell me?" He couldn't tell her now. She just informed him that she didn't feel that way towards him, but Bobby. He just looked at her and said, "I was….just going to tell you that I bet we both did really well on the big test we had today in Mrs. Benson's class."

"Oh, well I think I did pretty well. It wasn't as hard as I thought it would be. How about you?" she asked.

"OK I guess. We did study for it a lot."

"Yeah. Well, I'll see you later okay?" She took off running back towards the school; leaving Martin alone again, but this time, with his heart smashed down on the pavement.

The next day in school, Diana was standing with

Bobby at his locker, talking. Martin stood nearby watching where they couldn't see. It tore him up to see them together. Just then, Janet came up from behind Martin.

"There you are!" she said.

"I've been looking all over for you."

"Oh really?" he asked with pretend enthusiasm.

"Yes, I wanted to ask you to the Sadie Hawkins Dance." She was twirling her hair with her finger, like she did when she flirted with a boy.

"So will you come?" He glanced over at Diana and Bobby several lockers down and saw they were talking and obviously flirting with one another. It burned him up. He turned back to Janet.

"Sure, I'll go with you. Sounds like fun."

"Great!" she squealed. We can talk about it later. I've got to go to class now. Bye." She gave him a kiss on the cheek, just as Diana looked over and saw. Martin was watching Janet walk away and missed the hurt expression on Diana's face. It was the night of the big game and dance. The Tigers, which was Martin's team, were playing the Bobcats. The score was 14 to 9, in the fourth quarter. The Bobcats were winning. Martin wasn't playing his best. His mind wasn't on the game. He was upset about Diana going to the dance with Bobby. He just couldn't focus. Diana was standing with the other cheerleaders. Her back was towards Martin.

Team morale was low because the team was playing so lousy. Janet was standing behind where the Tiger team players were sitting and she blew Martin a kiss. Diana looked over in time to see it and stopped in mid-cheer. She didn't like seeing the way Janet was acting around Martin. For some reason, it made her mad. She couldn't quite figure it out, but she didn't like it. The Tigers coach called a time out, and the team huddled. Coach Morris was frustrated with his team. He could tell everyone was tired and so he needed to get them in a winning mood fast.

"Come on guys, I know you can play better than this! We've got to give it our best. I don't know what's bothering you," He said as he looked at Martin, "But you need to find that fight, that fire inside you and show the Bobcats what we're really made of. Now get your butts in gear and get back out there and let's win this game." He clapped his hands and the team members yelled.

"Yes Coach!" While Martin was huddling with his teammates, he looked over at Diana. Bobby had come over to talk with her and she looked up and saw that Martin was looking. She didn't know what compelled her to, but she grabbed Bobby and gave him a kiss on the cheek. This made Martin angry. Suddenly he found his fight, his fire. The clock had 10 seconds on it and the play began. Martin got back into position and waited until he could make his move. Suddenly the ball came his way. Martin grabbed it as it sailed towards him. With all the anger he had inside, he ran. An opponent tried to block him, but he pushed past them. One by one, they jumped to stop him, but he pushed as hard as he could and ran so fast they would fall behind his feet. The crowd was cheering. Diana looked away from Bobby to see what the commotion was all about. She saw Martin running towards the end zone with the ball.

"Run, Martin!" she yelled. Martin thought he heard Diana cheering for him, so he ran even faster. That was his fuel. The clock was down to four seconds, then three, two and as he finally reached the end zone, the clock buzzed. He had made a touchdown just in the nick of time. After the extra point was made, the Tigers had won the game, thanks to Martin. The scoreboard flashed 14 to 15. The crowd went wild. People were throwing confetti. Pom-poms were being shaken. The band began to play. The crowd began running onto the field towards the players. Martin was lifted up onto his team mates' shoulders. Diana ran onto the field towards him. She came up as he was lowered back down to his feet.

"That was great!" she said to him smiling. He decided he needed to tell her how he felt. No more wasting time.

"Thanks!" he said.

"Diana, I need to tell you something..... I." Just then, Janet pushed past Diana and threw her arms around Martin.

"You were wonderful, Babe!" she said. She grabbed his arm and pulled him away.

"Come on. I'll walk you to the locker room so you can change." She shot Diana a scornful look.

"It's almost time for our date for the dance." Martin turned back to look at Diana. He was about to say something but she was lost in the crowd. Diana stood there, watching Martin walk away with Janet on his arm. She realized that she envied Janet. Just then, Bobby walked up.

"Come on, we better get going to the dance before traffic gets really bad."

"Okay." She kept her gaze towards Martin, even though she could no longer see him.

"We're going to give Martin and Janet a ride to the dance." I promised her I would." he said.

"Oh Great!" she said under her breath. They went to the car and waited for Martin and Janet. In the locker room, the coach was giving a congratulations team speech. When it was over, and Martin had changed into jeans and a nice polo shirt, he found that Janet was outside the door waiting for him. She grabbed his arm.

"Bobby said him and Diana will give us a ride to the dance, isn't that nice of him?" Martin didn't answer. He didn't like the idea of seeing Diana and Bobby at the dance together, and he sure didn't like the idea of riding to the dance with them either. When Martin and Janet got to the car, Martin saw Diana sitting in the passenger seat. He didn't want to go to the stupid dance with Janet but what choice did he have? He could keep an eye on Diana and Bobby and make sure he didn't try something on her. They got in. Janet got in back with Martin. They all sat in silence at first and it was awkward. On the drive over, Janet and Bobby began talking which made it more awkward.

"Didn't Martin play great tonight?" Janet asked Bobby.

"Sure, whatever." he answered her keeping his eyes on the road while he drove.

"Oh, you're just jealous that you can't play!" Janet shot back at him with sarcasm.

"I could play if I wanted to." said Bobby.

"You don't know the first thing about playing the game." She said.

"Oh yeah? Well you would know about playing the game, you've played with almost every guy in school." Bobby was looking at her and back at the road. Janet was getting mad at Bobby.

"Liar!" she called him. She started climbing into the front seat between Diana and Bobby.

"Excuse me!" she said to Diana, pushing her over to the window. When she sat down between them, she continued her argument with Bobby.

"I only go out with guys that I like."

"You go out with any guy who asks you." Bobby said.

"Not true!"

"I can't remember how many guys you went out with."

"That doesn't surprise me, you couldn't even remember my birthday!" she said as he parked the car into a parking space behind the school. He turned off the car as he looked over at her.

"Wait, I remembered your birthday. I sent you flowers."

"I never got flowers." she wined.

"I must have given the wrong address or something. I paid like $50 bucks for them." Janet got quiet for a moment.

"You sent me flowers?" she asked him sweetly.

"Yes I did. I swear." he said back.

"Aw, that's so sweet, Bobby!" She leaned her head onto his shoulder.

"Come here and give me a kiss on the cheek," Bobby said to her. And she did.

"Bobby, let's not fight anymore." Diana looked at them and then in the back seat at Martin. She couldn't believe what was going on. They were making up, right during her and Bobby's date. Martin was trying not to laugh. Diana got out of the car and Martin did too. For a moment, they were silent while Bobby and Janet were still in the car talking. But then, Diana spoke up.

"They really deserve each other!" The both laughed.

"Martin, I'm really sorry for the way I've been these past few days. I don't know what's come over me. I've just been going through some things I'm trying to deal with." Martin answered.

"I know what you mean. Besides, Mike's death is still fresh on our minds. I guess it will be a while before things go back to normal for us all." Diana smiled.

"Yeah, I guess that's it. Hey, you were going to tell me something earlier on the field. What was it?" Martin suddenly chickened out again. He didn't think now was quite the time, since she seemed still a mess with her emotions. It would have to wait for the right time when they were alone, or he could blow the whole thing and she could end up mad. Instead, he simply said, "You look nice tonight." She smiled a big smile.

"Really? It's just my cheerleading outfit. I didn't get the chance to change."

"Well, It looks nice on you." he said with a shy smile. She smiled too.

"Thanks!" They walked into the gym where the dance was taking place. Bobby and Janet were holding hands behind them. Inside, students were packed on the dance floor while a fast song was playing. Bobby turned to Diana.

"Sorry about our date. Janet and I just needed to talk about things. I hope you understand." Janet turned to him.

"Sure she does, we belong together. We never should have broken up. Now come on and let's dance." They walked onto the dance floor and left Diana and Martin standing there. They stood for a moment in awkward silence. The music turned from a fast song to a slow one. Martin walked up to Diana and held out his arm to her.

"Would you care to dance, miss?" he asked her. She smiled and giggled.

"Why, yes I would! She took his arm. Together they moved onto the dance floor. They slow-danced without talking for a moment. Martin was holding her in his arms and his heart was beating fast. He was so close to telling her how he felt! He was trying to get up the courage, when she began talking to him.   She smiled up at him.

"You played great tonight." He returned her smile.

"Thanks." He wanted to tell her that it was all for her.

"I'm sorry about you and Bobby." he said, even though he really wasn't. He was glad that Janet and Bobby were back together. It had been killing him that Diana liked Bobby.

"Well, I guess it's for the best that they get back together. They are perfect for each other. They're both shallow and don't have a clue." Martin and Diana began to laugh.

"I'm glad you're here." she told Martin.

"I could really use a friend." She put her head on his shoulder. She felt wonderful in his arms. He wanted desperately to lift up her head and kiss her lips. It was killing him inside, holding back. But he had to. He didn't want to ruin their friendship. Mike had tried to take her friendship farther and she refused. All that mattered was that she was in his arms with her head on his shoulders. He never wanted that song to stop playing. He wanted to stay that way with her forever. Even if he would be nothing more than a friend to her, he'd take what he could get. Besides, she was in his arms regardless. After the dance, Martin and Diana walked home together. They talked about how nice the dance was, about how weird the Bobby and Janet situation was, and how they missed Mike.

"Too bad Mike couldn't have been there. He would have enjoyed seeing you make a touchdown." Diana said.

"So tell me something." he asked her.

"Did you ever kiss Mike?" Diana was surprised by that question and looked up at him. She thought for a moment, and smiled.

"No. I mean not besides the kiss on the cheek I gave him in the hospital. He tried more than once to kiss me, but I wasn't ready. It didn't seem right with him, you know what I mean? I mean we were such good friends and all, it just would have been a bad idea." Martin heard all he needed to hear and was glad that he didn't tell her how he felt. She was pretty much making it clear by what she was saying that they were just friends, just like Mike and she were, and that any attempt from him to make it more would be a disaster. As hard as it would be, he would have to keep his secret. They arrived in front of their houses. He walked her to her door. Neither one of their parents were home because they both worked the second shift.

"It's been an interesting evening." She said.

"Yes it has." he answered. She gave him a hug.

"I better get inside. I promised Dad I would be home by 10 and he said he would call just to make sure." Martin bowed in front of her and said with an English accent, "Good evening, ma'am. It's been a pleasure." She laughed and gave a curtsy.

"Good evening, kind sir." she said. They both gave a little giggle and held their gaze with one another.

"Well, I better go." she said. She opened up the door and went inside, leaving Martin alone on the porch. After a moment, he turned, walked home and went inside. As he closed the door behind him, he leaned back on it. He was going to have to be stronger if he was going to keep his feelings for her inside. He had almost told her. That would have ruined everything. Martin sat down on the couch and turned on the TV. He had watched about a half hour of a movie, when the phone rang. Expecting his mom, he was surprised when he heard Diana on the other line sobbing.

"Diana, calm down." he said.

"I can't understand what you're saying." She was wheezing.

"I can't breathe, please help me!"

"I'll be right there." He put down the phone and ran out the door. A moment later, he burst into her front door. He found her still in her cheerleading outfit, lying on the floor. He ran to her and knelt down.

"Diana, Diana answer me!" he cried. She didn't answer. She was unconscious. He quickly ran for the phone and dialed 9-11. When the dispatcher answered, he quickly spoke up.

"Please help me. My friend had an asthma attack. She... She's unconscious. I don't know what to do!"

"Do you know CPR?" the dispatcher asked him.

"A little, I've seen it done before." He was sitting by her in a panic.

"Okay, good!" the dispatcher said.

"Is she breathing? Put your ear up to her nose. Do you feel a breath?" He did that and felt nothing.

"No, I don't think she is.. I can't tell!" The dispatcher spoke up.

"Okay. What's your name?"

"Mm... Martin." he said.

"Okay, Martin, It'll be okay. I'll tell you what to do. Lift up the back of her neck and tilt her head back to open her airway." He did that.

"Now put your mouth over hers, hold her nose and blow your breath into her lungs two times and see if her chest rises."

"Okay, hold on." he said and put the phone down. He pinched softly on her nose and put his mouth up to hers, opened her mouth, and blew two long breaths. He saw her chest move up and down each time. He grabbed up the phone quickly and said frantically, "Okay now what?"

"You need to put your ear down over her mouth and nose. See if you can hear any breathing." He put his ear near her mouth and listened. He heard a very faint sound but couldn't feel a breath.

"I can't tell! Oh God what do I do?"

"If there is no breath, you need to continue with the breaths. Keep breathing for her until the paramedics get there. Do you understand?"

"Yeah, I got it." he answered.

"They're almost there, Martin, just hang in there."

"Okay" Martin said. He put the phone down, and pinched her nose closed and gave her two breaths. She wasn't responding. He continued the process again saying, "Please breathe Diana, come on. Breathe!" He was breathing for her as tears ran down his face.

"Please breathe! he kept repeating. He wasn't about to give up on her. He put his face next to her mouth to hear if she was breathing. Very faint sounds.

"Please Diana, Don't die on me, please!" he was sobbing.

"I love you Diana, Please don't die!" Suddenly she took a breath. Martin held his as he waited for her to take another one. She did and started breathing normally on her own.

"Oh, thank God!" Martin said as he leaned back and wiped away his tears. She started coughing. With one hand, he held hers and brushed away the hair from her face with his other one. With her eyes still closed she made a small sound.

"Martin..."

"I'm right here! You're gonna be okay." Just then the paramedics came and quickly went over to Martin

"Good work, son. We'll take it from here." one of the paramedics said. They gave her a shot to help her breath better. It seemed to help. Martin got out of the way as they lifted her up onto the gurney, and checked her heartbeat and blood pressure. They wheeled her outside and raised her into the back of the ambulance

"I want to ride in with her!" Martin said. It wasn't a question. He was pretty much demanding it. The paramedic wasn't going to argue with the boy that just saved her life and they let him sit in back with her as they drove her to the hospital. They made Martin wait out in the waiting area as the doctors took care of Diana. Her dad was called at work and he soon arrived. When he saw Martin in the waiting area, he hurried over.

"How is she?" he asked Martin.

"I think she's fine now, but they won't let me go in."

"I'm going in to see her. I'll let you know." Martin nodded his head. James went over to the desk and asked the receptionist where his daughter Diana Taylor's room was. The receptionist typed on a keyboard and looked up the room number and then spoke up.

"She's in 408. I'll buzz you in." She pushed a button on the desk and a door opened. He went inside. A moment later, Teresa walked up to Martin, who was pacing the floor.

"I checked on her a minute ago and she's doing fine, thanks to you." she said with a smile. She knew Martin was worried.

"Is she going to be okay?" he asked.

"Well, why don't you go in and ask her yourself?" she asked him.

"You mean I can go in?" he asked her with wide eyes.

"Well, I'm the head nurse and I say it's okay. If anyone has any problems with it, they'll have to deal with me." she said. They exchanged smiles. She led him down to Diana's room. When he went in, Diana was sitting up while Dr. Peterson and James were quietly talking in the corner. They stopped talking when Martin came in with his mom. Diana looked over and when she saw Martin, her eyes lit up.

"Martin!" she said as he walked in. He quickly walked over and stood on the opposite side of Diana's bed, across from James and the doctor. Teresa walked up and stood by him.

"We'll, if you need anything, just buzz for the nurse." said Dr. Peterson.

"Okay, thanks doctor." Diana said, as he walked out of the room.

"How are you feeling?" Martin asked her.

"Fine now, thanks to you." she said with a smile. James looked up from his daughter and looked at Martin.

"We're glad you were there to help her. She wouldn't be here with us if you hadn't been there for her. We're both truly grateful." James brushed his fingers across Diana's cheek and she smiled up at him.

"You're a great friend to her. I'm proud of you, Martin." James told him.

"I'm proud of you too!" Teresa said. She put her hand on Martin's shoulder.

"By the way, how did both your dates go tonight?" she asked them. Martin and Diana looked at each other and smiled.

"Oh, it was interesting!" said Diana with a smile. She made a small cough. Teresa said, "Okay, we better let you get your rest, young lady. You've had quite an evening."

"Alright." Diana said. Martin and his mom waved goodbye to Diana and started walking out of her room. James came up behind Martin.

"Martin, can I talk to you for a minute?" he asked.

"Sure." Martin answered.

"Martin, I'll be waiting in the car." Teresa told him and walked away to leave James and Martin to talk privately. They were standing just outside of Diana's room where she couldn't hear them.

"I want to thank you again for being there for her tonight." He reached out to shake Martin's hand. Martin grabbed it and they shook.

"It was nothing, Mr. Taylor. She would have done the same for me."

"She sure would." James agreed.

"Dr. Peterson told me tonight that the weather and allergies here are bad for her asthma. He really suggests that she move away." Martin's smile was fading.

"Her mother lives in San Francisco. She's been wanting Diana to come live with her for a while now. There is an excellent specialist there that could give Diana better care than here. I hate to say it, but Diana would probably be better off there. If you hadn't been there for her tonight, to save her, she wouldn't be alive now. I just can't take that chance again." James lowered his head.

"She means the world to me, Martin. If it could mean her life, I know we both will agree that she should go." James looked back at Martin who was now frowning with his head down. He didn't want to let Diana go.

"Martin, I want you to do me a favor. When I tell her about this, she isn't going to want to move away and leave her father and her best friend behind. I know her. She's sweet, but stubborn that way. I need you to do your best to talk her into going." Martin couldn't believe what he was hearing. He hated the idea of her going away; moving away from him. She was his world, his reason for getting up in the morning. She was the smile on his face, and now he was the one who would have to convince her to move away from him. It was the hardest thing he had ever been asked to do.

"Martin, I know how hard this is for you. But can I count on you with this?" James asked him. Martin took a moment to take it all in. He knew what he had to do, as painful as it was. He cared for her so much that he had to let her go. He swallowed hard. He looked up from the floor and saw tears in James's eyes. He knew it was just as hard for James to let Diana go as it was for him.

"Sure, Mr. Taylor, I'll do my best." he said, trying to be strong. James gave him a half smile, pulled him in and gave him a quick hug.

"Thanks, Martin. I know it's asking a lot." And with that, James walked back into Diana's room. It was asking a lot. James had no idea just how much he was asking. Martin cherished Diana. He had since he first saw her in the window the night she was practicing her singing. This had turned out to be the worst night for him since his dad died. He kept losing the people he cared about in his life. When Martin got home, he waved goodbye to his mother as she left to go back to work at the hospital. He went straight to bed and cried himself to sleep.

Chapter Seven

The night before Diana moved was just about the hardest thing Martin had ever gone through, with the exception of his dad's death. Diana and Martin lay side-by-side on her trampoline looking up at the starry sky. They both just laid in silence for a long time, neither one of them saying a word. Finally, Diana spoke up.

"Martin?"

"Yeah?"

"What do think is up there? Do you think there are other people looking down at us wondering if we really exist?" Martin giggled a little."Yeah. I think there has to be more than just us out here. The universe is so huge that there has to be more out there."

"Yeah, I guess you're right." Just then she spotted a shooting star streak across the sky.

"Oh! A shooting star!" She pointed at it and he saw it too.

"Quickly! We have to make a wish!" They both closed their eyes tightly for a moment.

"What was your wish?" she asked him.

"Oh, I can't tell you or it won't come true."

"Oh, fair enough!" she said There was a pause. Then he spoke again.

"I'll tell you when the time is right!" he said with a smile.

"What about you? What did you wish for?"

"I wished that no matter where we both are, that we'll always be best friends and that both our dreams come true. That I become a famous singer and you become a pilot." Martin smiled.

"That's a great wish!" Martin?"

"Mm-hmm?"

"What's it like up there, flying?" He sat up.

"Oh it's amazing! My dad took me flying on a plane several times. It's like the world just fades away and you become one with the clouds and sky. You forget everything else!" She sat up.

"I want to be up there right now, forgetting the world! I just can't believe I'm leaving tomorrow."

"Me either." Martin said sadly.

"This has been my home as long as I can remember. My dad is here, my best friend is here, and my school is here. I don't want to leave you all behind. I miss my mom, and I'm glad that I get to see her, but I haven't seen her in four years. What if I don't like her? What if she doesn't like me?" She put her head down on Martin's shoulder and began to cry. He lifted up her face with his hand on her chin.

"She is gonna love you, and you are gonna love her. California is great. You're going to love it there, trust me! The summers are nice and warm, not like here where it's so humid everything sticks to you. And the winters are hardly cold, just rainy a lot sometimes. It'll be fine, you'll see." he said to her. He was trying to lift her spirits and make her open to the idea of moving to California, while inside, he wanted to hold on to her and never let her go. Being brave was hard on him, but he was doing it for her. He didn't want her to have another bad asthma attack again. He knew it could be fatal for her. Her life was so precious to him. She was his everything, and even if it meant being away from her, he wanted her to be healthy.

"I don't want to leave you." she told him.

"You're the best friend I have ever had." He wiped the tears off her cheek.

"As soon as I'm out of boot camp, I'm going to put in for orders to Camp Pendleton. Then we will be really close to each other, and we can visit whenever we want. Then I'll take you up in my plane." He smiled at her. She put her hand over his.

"Promise?" He looked deep into her eyes.

"I swear." he said. Diana and Martin looked at each other for a moment in silence. Suddenly she spoke up.

"I don't have to go. We can run away tonight, you and me! If Daddy can't find me I won't have to go."

"No Diana, you have to go." Martin said sternly.

"But you don't want me to go, I know. He looked at her confused.

"What do you mean?"

"You told me you loved me, the night of my asthma attack. I was almost unconscious, but I heard it. You said it, didn't you?" Martin was so confused. He did love her with all his heart but he knew she needed to go. If he told her the truth, she wouldn't go. She'd want to stay with him, and as much as he wanted that, he knew she needed to go. She was looking deep into his eyes searching for an answer. He looked back at her and with what little strength he had said, "You're my best friend! I was scared. I didn't want to lose you! I don't remember what I was saying then." She was shaking her head at him.

"I could have sworn you said it. Maybe I'm wrong." After a pause, she looked over and looked him right in the eyes.

"Do you?" He had to stay strong. This wasn't about him. This was about her getting better. She was everything to him but he could never forgive himself if he told her the truth and she stayed. Her asthma would get worse. She could even die, and his selfishness would be to blame. He shook his head as he tried to stay strong.

"You're my best friend Diana!"

"Answer the question. Do you love me?" Yes he loved her! Deep inside his heart was crying out. His heart was breaking as he said the words he didn't mean.

"I don't know! All I know is that I lost my dad, Mike, and now I'm losing you! Maybe I'm numb, or confused. I'm sorry Diana, but I don't know how I feel." Her expression grew grim. After a moment of disbelief and hurt, she started to cry, and quickly got up, climbed off the trampoline, and ran toward home. He didn't want her to go off like that.

"Diana!" he yelled. She stopped and turned to him.

"What Martin! What can you say that will make this all be better? What can you tell me that will take away the hurt I feel leaving you, my dad, my friends and my home?" She waited for an answer from him. He wanted desperately to tell her he loved her. He wanted more than anything to say it. But he loved her too much and couldn't say it. He let out a deep sigh and after a long pause. He said

"I'm sorry Diana." With that, she looked down, turned, and ran inside. He wanted to call to her to come back but he just let her leave. As soon as she was out of sight, he felt like dying. What had he done? Was this a mistake? She was reaching out to him for his love and he had denied her. He knew that he was doing the right thing but at a horrible price. The next day James and Teresa were talking by his car. Diana put the last of her bags in the trunk and stood by the car door. She looked over her shoulder at Martin, who was just sitting on the porch. She turned back around.

"Diana, I'll miss you sweetheart." Teresa said as she gave Diana a hug.

"I'll miss you too, Ms. Davis." Diana said to her. Diana looked over at Martin and gave him a sad look. He just looked down. Both Teresa and James noticed the silence between the two teens. James spoke up.

"Diana, before I take you to the airport, don't you want to say goodbye to Martin?" Without a word she sat in the car and shut the door, never looking at Martin. Martin would not look at her, he acted like she wasn't there. Both James and Teresa exchanged puzzled looks at each other.

"Well, I guess this is it." James said.

"Drive safely to the airport." Teresa said to him. James said goodbye to Martin who waved back at him. James got in the car and after a heavy sigh, he turned the car on and started backing up. He turned onto the street and started to drive away. Teresa stood waving. Suddenly the car stopped and Diana's door came open. She jumped out.

"Martin!" He stood up when he heard her and started running towards her. She ran towards him crying. When they met they put their arms around each other tight. They just stood there for a long time just holding each other. Finally she spoke up.

"I'll write you every day! I'll tell you all about my mother and everything I do."

"I'll write to you every day too! Even from boot camp and from wherever they send me after that!" She and Martin locked their eyes on each other, hardly turning their eyes away as she walked back to the car and got inside. She waved at him and he waved back. He was wiping away tears. She looked back at him from the back window of the car. As he watched her car pull away down the street, his heart sank into his chest but he never took his eyes off of her until she was out of sight. Suddenly Martin and his mom were left standing in the street alone. Martin felt like his heart stopped beating.

A tear fell down his cheek. Half his heart just took off for California, leaving him behind. But he knew he was going to see her again. He made a vow to himself that he was going to carry out his promise to Diana and move to California as soon as he finished boot camp. Then, he would be a man, she would be a woman, and he would do his best to win her heart for his own; to truly tell her how he felt and not hide it.

November 14, 1981

Dear Martin,

Hi, how are you? Well, I'm here in San Francisco. The weather here is nice, just like you said. As soon as I got off the plane, I was breathing so much better. Mom is nice. She was waiting for me when I got off the plane. We recognized each other right off and ran into each other's arms. She's just as beautiful as I remembered her being. Her house is fantastic. I wish you could see it. It's right on the beach.

Mom's house, I mean my new home is really big. I've never been in a big home before in my life. Mom has a maid and a butler just like you see on TV. The butler here is Myles and the maid is Lucy. They both are very nice. Myles is English and he is funny. He likes to tell jokes and he even played baseball when he was younger. He told me he is going to take me to a game soon.

Lucy is more like a big sister to me. She makes sure I clean up after myself which I should do anyways and not expect her to do. I feel weird when she has to clean up after me even though cleaning is her job. I need to be responsible for my own messes. Mom, on the other hand doesn't clean up after herself. I guess she has gone so long having Lucy do it that she is so dependent on her. You should see my room. It's gorgeous and so big! It's kind of creepy at night though because it seems so big and empty then. Mom and I had our first dinner together in the grand dining room but I much prefer to eat in the kitchen where the table isn't so big. Mom and I almost have to shout across the table to talk. Well, really I talk. She is usually reading the paper or on the phone with her agent. But we did go to the movies together yesterday and out to dinner. Today, she took me to the theater with her and I got to see her on stage. She's great! I wish you could meet her. You would like her. I miss you and Dad. I miss playing baseball with the guys. I miss our school too. I even miss Randy's funny remarks when he strikes out.

I hope everything is fine where you are. Are you keeping up your grades? I start my first day of school tomorrow. I'm nervous about being new at school.

Myles is going to drive me each morning and pick me up. It's not far and I'd rather walk but mom insists that I would get too much sun. Life sure is different here. I guess I just need time to get used to it all. I better get to bed; it's 9:08 pm here. You are three hours ahead of me, I think. I can't remember. Well, I hope you are doing fine. I wrote like I promised I would. Are you and the guys still playing baseball in the field? Tell the guys I said hi. I miss you lots!

Sincerely,
Diana

November 25, 1981

Dear Diana,

I got your letter the other day and was excited to hear from you. I'm glad that you are breathing better and that you and your mother are getting along great. I'm sorry she doesn't have much time to spend with you but hopefully she will soon. Yes, we still play baseball out in the field. Chris and the guys say hi. School is going okay. It's been hard keeping up my grades with my study partner gone. We're having a Christmas dance next month. I don't know if I will go though.

Remember Stephanie Reed, from the cheer leading squad? Well she asked me to go with her, but I don't know. We are winning most of our football games. We played the Eagles from Huntsville High last week and we wiped the floor with them. Janet and Bobby broke up and made up again twice since you left. My mom is now working the day shift, so I get to see her more. We went out to dinner the other night and bumped into your dad. He said he misses you dearly but is happy that you are doing so well there. Mom and your dad have decided to go out on a date. Isn't that funny? I guess they both are tired of being lonely. So, have you met any famous people yet? I bet it won't be long until you are singing and acting in a movie. Will you remember me when you make it big? You'll do fine at your new school. Soon you'll have lots of friends to write to me about.

The way that I made it through the first day of school was because of you. I miss you. I better stop writing now, my hand is cramping up and I've got homework. Write soon. Happy Thanksgiving!

Sincerely,

Martin

December 16, 1981

Dear Martin,

School is going fine here. I have made so many new friends. Katherine is my best friend, besides you, of course. We have all our classes together. I have told her about you. She wishes she could meet you. I told Mom all about you too. I have been seeing an asthma specialist here and he has me on new medicine. So far, so good. I don't see mom very much. She is usually at the theater most of the day, or out at parties. We do have breakfast together.

I started up voice lessons with a top instructor from Los Angeles, and mom wants me to start taking acting lessons. It sounds like fun. I have been taking drama in school. I like it. We're doing a Christmas musical next week. I tried out and guess what? I got the lead part! I about fell over when I heard. Isn't that great? I'm so excited about it. I'm still in shock. Boy, I've got so many lines to memorize before opening night! I guess I better get memorizing. I hope you are doing fine. Take care. Merry Christmas, and happy New Year!

Yours truly,

Diana P.S. Stephanie Reed is a sweet girl; you should take her to the dance. Have fun and tell me how it goes.

January 12, 1982

Diana, Hi, it's me. Well, I went to the dance with Stephanie. We had a pretty good time. She seems pretty nice. But we are just friends. She's not really my type and when you have your heart set on a certain type of person, no one else will do. Christmas was okay here. I got some nice things. Mostly clothes, though. Your dad and my mom are dating exclusively now. I guess that means they are getting pretty serious. They go out at least twice a week. Mom is happier than I've seen her in a while.

All the guys ask about you. I told them how you're going to be a big star soon. They said not to forget them. I'm glad you got the big part in your play. I wish I could have been there to see it. I'm sure you sang wonderfully. I can't wait till June 3rd. That's when I turn 16. Mom took me to get my drivers permit yesterday. Now, I want to drive everywhere. I hope you had a great Christmas and New Year. Please write soon. I miss you!

Your Friend,

Martin

July 5th, 1982

Dear Martin,

How are you? I'm sorry that I don't get the chance to write you very often. I will try to be better about it. You're my best friend and we need to keep in-touch all the time. We had a wonderful Fourth of July picnic yesterday. Mom and me went and sat on the beach with a picnic basket and ate fried chicken, macaroni and cheese, biscuits and watermelon, and when the sun went down, we saw the fireworks going off in the distance. It was so peaceful. I bet you played baseball with the guys in the field, didn't you? That was always a Fourth of July tradition in the neighborhood. Well, I guess I better go. Write soon!

Yours truly,

Diana

November 2, 1982

Dear Diana,

How is life in California? It's pretty normal here. School is going fine. I don't get to hear from you very much. I hope you haven't forgotten about me since you have so much going on in your life.

Mr. Benson had a heart attack last week in class and passed away. He was in the middle of grading papers when he grabbed his chest and hit the floor. Everyone is in shock. He was a pretty healthy man. His wife said he ran four miles every day. I guess it must have been a hidden condition. It's a shame. He was my favorite teacher. Mom let me start flying lessons six months ago.

Guess what? I got my private pilot license. I can fly a small plane but not jets yet. Well, I just wanted to say hi. Please write soon!

With love,

Martin

February 7th, 1983

Dear Martin,

I am so sorry I haven't written you back in so long! I am so busy! I have voice lessons, acting lessons, modeling, school and an after school job as a waitress going on all at once.

Guess what? I put in an application for the School of Performing Arts in New York. I sure hope I get in. I should hear something soon. Graduation is three and a half months away. I can't believe I won't be graduating with you. I was sorry to hear about Mr. Benson. I liked him too. I guess it proves that you never know when God will call on you.

I bought my first car. It's a used one. It's not much, but it gets me from place to place. I'm so excited for you that you got your private pilot's license! Congrats! I haven't forgotten your promise, ya know! I expect a ride soon! I'm glad your mom and my dad are getting along so well. Do you think they will end up getting married? Doesn't that seem weird? Ha Ha!

Love ya!

Diana

December 25th 1983

Diana,

Merry Christmas! I wanted to take a moment from the Christmas craze to wish you a merry Christmas. Mom is making her famous ham and sweet potatoes. She invited over James and half the staff from the hospital. She also invited Mike's parents. They are trying to patch things up. I sure hope they do. I know Mike would have wanted them to stay together.

I don't know how much time I'm going to have before all the guests get here so I thought if I were going to write you, I had better do it before anyone arrives. It's pretty cold here. I know you must be enjoying Christmas with your mom. You probably have been hitting Rodeo Drive pretty hard huh? Just kidding. Well, my thoughts are with you. Please write soon. Keep in touch!

With love,

Martin

February 6th 1984

Martin,

How are you? I am still waiting to hear if I got accepted to the School or Performing Arts. I am looking forward to graduation in a few months, I'm excited about what's in store for me after, but I sure miss being back in South Carolina. I'm feeling homesick more and more. I don't get to spend much time with Mom and with all I've got going on, I really miss you and wish you could come for a visit. At least my asthma is so much better. I don't get to have much free time and I sure would give anything to play another game of baseball with you guys again.

Miss you!

Diana

June 3, 1984

Diana,

Hi. I wish I could come visit you. Well, I graduated two weeks ago. I'm so glad to be out of school. Chris and I went cruising in my car all evening after the ceremony. We hit the town. It was a blast. I went and signed up for the Marine Corps today since it's my 18th birthday. I start boot camp in two and a half weeks. The physical exam was something strange. A bunch of us guys standing around in line in our boxers while strangers look us over up and down. I guess that's how they root out who's worthy to be Marine material. I am excited and nervous about it at the same time. I know it's pretty rough in boot camp.

My mom tried to talk me out of it last week but she couldn't. I want to be a pilot and so that's what I'm gonna do. I guess you heard that your dad and my mom no longer are dating. I think he wanted something a little too serious than what she is ready for. I don't think she ever got over Dad. She must not think that she could ever love like that again. I want her to be happy, she deserves it. I thought I'd never say this but I want her to find someone she can love again. I haven't seen your dad since they broke up, about five months ago. He moved to another area of base housing.

Did you make it in the performing arts school you applied to? I hope so. You are so talented! I hope you are doing fine. Chris and I are going to live it up until I go to boot camp. There are still baseball games in the field, but not all the old players. Randy got married, can you believe it? Him and Karen Sims. They got married the day after graduation. He has really mellowed out since you left. He actually turned out to be sort of a gentleman once Karen caught his attention. He quit swearing so much and started dressing up preppy. He did a complete turn-around. Even started going to church if you can believe that. He must really love her. Mike's dad took down the tree house. It was falling apart anyways. No one was really using it except to take their girlfriends up there to make out. He and Mike's mom worked things out and he even stopped drinking. They started counseling and guess what? They had a baby five months ago. A girl. They named her Rebecca. She's a pretty baby.

Mike would have made a fuss over her if he could have seen her. She looks so much like him. But small and girly. Most of the other guys are off doing their own thing. It's a new group of kids that play ball back there now. Your secret fishing spot is still there. I don't think any of the new kids have discovered it yet. Well, that's it for now I guess. I'll write you while I'm in boot camp.

Love,

Martin

June 3, 1984

Dear Martin,

Happy Birthday! I just wanted to send you a letter on your birthday letting you know I remembered. Life is so busy for me I can hardly get any rest. Mom has been traveling so I haven't seen her in weeks. It get's lonely here by myself sometimes. Luckily Myles likes to play checkers too. Write soon!

Love,

Diana

July 13, 1984

Dear Diana,

Mom cried when I left for boot camp. It was hard leaving her, but here I am at boot camp. From the moment you get off the bus they are yelling at you. In fact, they haven't stopped yelling. You can even hear them in your sleep. Well, what little sleep you get. They get us up before the sun and start yelling at you then.

Chow is challenging. As soon as you get your tray and sit, you only have until the last guy sits down with his tray to eat. As soon as he sits, you are done, whether or not you actually ate. I've lost five lbs since I arrived here because they hardly give you time to eat. Rule to remember, never be that last guy or you'll go hungry. A typical day consists of getting up early, eat breakfast as fast as possible, hoping you aren't last in line. Then we do exercises. We then jog three miles around camp. Then we stop to eat lunch, avoiding being the last guy, then we run the obstacle course for a few hours.

After that, we eat dinner. Again not being that guy. We get about an hour of personal time to shower, write letters, or see the doctor, then it's lights out. It's very difficult to go through, but being a Marine is what I want. Just like everything else in life, you have to take the bad with the good.

I met a guy here who wants to be a pilot too! His name is Oliver Warren. He's from Savannah Georgia, not too far from Beaufort. Small world huh? He's requesting to be stationed at Camp Pendleton too! I hope we both get to. That would be very cool! Well, I only have a few minutes left to send this letter out, so I have to make this letter short. I wish that you could come to my boot camp graduation, but I understand if you won't be able to make it. I miss you and hope that we will see each other soon.

With love,

Martin

It was a week away from boot camp graduation. Martin was out on the rifle range. He was lying on the ground with his rifle pointed down range. He was trying to concentrate on the target up ahead. Next to him was his buddy Warren who was loading his rifle. Martin had gotten a letter from Diana earlier that day and he was waiting until he was alone to read it. He had put it in his pocket and didn't notice that it had fallen out while he was on the ground, until Warren spoke up.

"Hey Davis, what's this?" Warren reached down, grabbed it and stood up holding the letter. Martin looked over and saw what Warren had.

"Is this a letter from a girl?" Warren teased. Martin stood up, tried to grab the letter from his buddy but Warren held it away from him.

"It smells like it!" Warren teased as he sniffed it.

"Is she pretty?" Martin grinned.

"She's beautiful."

"Nice! Is she your girl?" Martin smiled again.

"No. She's just a really good friend."

"Let me guess, you want it to be more, right?" Martin wondered if it was too obvious.

"I know how it is. I've been there. You've just got to get her out of your mind, unless in her letter, she's confessing her undying love for you." They both smiled. Warren was about to give it back to Martin when Drill Sergeant Miller came up behind him.

"Ten-Hut!" The two of them stood at attention with the rest of the platoon.

"What's this?" asked Drill Sergeant Miller.

"Do you two recruits think you're so good at taking out the enemy that you don't have to train with the rest of your platoon?" Hiding the letter by his side, Warren spoke up.

"Sir, no Sir!" The Sergeant looked over at Martin who was looking ahead at attention.

"What about you recruit? You better than the rest of your platoon? Should I just step aside and let you do the training?" Martin spoke up.

"Sir, no Sir!" Just then the sergeant looked over and saw that Warren was hiding something.

"What's this we have here, recruit?" Warren paused but then answered.

"Sir, nothing Sir!"

"Nothing? How stupid do you think I am boy? Looks to me like you've got a letter. Well boy, I don't get love letters from recruits very often. Go ahead and open it up and read it to me! Touch me in the feels!" Warren knew that Martin's letter was probably personal and felt horrible that he had taken it from his buddy. Warren paused.

"But Sir, I..." he stuttered.

"Now recruit, or do you want the rest of your platoon to do 50 push-ups in the mud on your behalf?" the sergeant growled. Warren glanced at Martin, gave him an expression of apology, then slowly opened up the letter, cleared his throat nervously, and began to read aloud.

"Dear Martin, how is boot camp? Are they treating you good there? I got your letter and wrote right away. I have two great things to tell you. First, I got accepted at the School of Performing Arts in New York! I just about fell through the floor when I got my acceptance letter. I start going in three months." Warren stopped reading and looked up. Martin smiled. Yes! She made it! Martin thought to himself! He was so proud of her.

"Keep reading recruit! We're all entertained, aren't we boys?" the Sergeant said sarcastically. A few of the guys chuckled. Warren looked over at Martin who was standing just looking forward irritated. Martin wanted to punch out the sergeant for making Warren read her letter out-loud. Warren continued reading.

"The other thing may surprise you. But guess what? I have met someone and we're getting married. His name is Jake Stein..." Martin's heart seemed to stop as Warren read those words. He just stood there looking forward. His expression was like stone. Warren stopped reading and looked over at Martin. He knew this wasn't great news for him. Martin didn't move. Just stood there looking forward. Warren very discreetly whispered over to him.

"Oh I'm so sorry man. I didn't mean to.." Just then the sergeant spoke up.

"Okay! The show's over. Everyone pick up your gear. You boys wanna go eat, don't you? Now move out!" The Sergeant walked off. Everyone got out of formation and started picking up their gear. It began to rain. Martin just stood there, looking forward as the rain fell. He was grateful that it began to rain. No one would notice his eyes welling up. Warren saw that Martin was still standing there.

"You okay?" Still looking forward, Martin spoke up.

"I'm fine! I'm happy for her!"   He turned to Warren, looked at him for a moment, grabbed the letter from his hand, and without saying another word, he turned and walked away. Later that evening, Martin lay in his bunk holding her letter. He looked at it in his hands for a moment. Then finally he decided to finish reading what she had written.

Jake and I perform together at the local theater. I met him there. I played his wife in a musical. We had chemistry right off. You would like him, Martin. I told him all about you. He is going to the Performing Arts School too. We've been dating for five months now and it got pretty serious. He popped the question last month. I know it all seems so sudden. I can hardly believe it myself. Can you believe a big time guy from L.A. wants to marry a silly tomboy from South Carolina?

I have a favor to ask. I know you probably won't be able to, but I want you to walk me down the aisle. Daddy won't do it. He doesn't approve of the wedding, saying I'm way too young, but I know you aren't like that. I know you would understand. Please come if you can. I can't think of anyone else I'd rather have be there for me than you. Please say you will. It's going to be in Manhattan on September 11th. I'll send you the address. I wish I could come to your graduation but I just can't get away. So much going on but I'll be thinking of you. I'm so proud of you! Keep in touch!

With Love,

Diana

He couldn't believe it. She was getting married. How could she marry another man? he thought to himself. He was the one who loved her for so long. He's the one whose heart sank when she moved away. No one else could ever love her as much as he did. Yet, she seemed to have found the man she wanted to marry. It wasn't him. He wanted to go to that wedding, march up to this Jake person and say, "How dare you take her away? How dare you steal her heart when she belongs with me? She's had my heart for so long and you come along and take hers away and claim it as your own."

For weeks, he had waited for her to write him, and when she finally did, she wrote telling him how she was going to marry someone else. She had broken his heart into. Everything he did was for her, and she was hurting him more than anyone ever could. Didn't she know how he felt? How could she know? He lied to her the night before she moved away.

That was such a mistake and now he is paying for it. He knew he should have told her how he felt that night Even though she thought of him as just a friend, he should have showed her how he felt. Maybe, just maybe she'd be marrying him and not this Jake person. Someone else was holding her, kissing her. She was going to spend the rest of her life with this other guy. Maybe even have kids with him. Kids that should be theirs. Martin looked up and saw Warren walking up to him.

"Hey, Davis, you doing okay? I'm really sorry about reading your letter. The drill sergeant is such a jerk." Martin, without taking his eyes off the letter spoke up.

"That's okay man. Don't worry about it." Warren stood for a moment, then said

"Some of the guys are getting a card game started in a minute. Are you coming?" Martin shook his head and put the letter down on the bed beside him and draped his arm over his eyes.

"I'm exhausted! I'm turning in."

"Okay man, I'll catch you later." and with that, his buddy walked away leaving him alone in his grief. That night Martin hardly got any sleep. He just lay on the bed and stared at the ceiling for hours. He felt like he had no ambition in life anymore. That Jake Stein had taken it all away.

Chapter Eight

Martin was dressed in his uniform, standing in formation at his boot camp graduation. His mom was in the bleachers taking pictures of him. She took out a handkerchief and wiped the tears away from her eyes. She was so proud of her son. The years had flown by and she couldn't believe this day was here. The day was hot and sunny. The ceremony was just about over. Staff Sergeant Miller called out

"PLATOON 1054, DISMISSED!" The platoon responded with

"AYE STAFF SERGEANT." They did an About Face and yelled OOH RAH!" Then it was over and the crowd began clapping. After they were dismissed, the new Marines broke off into little huddles while family members crowded around their sons, brothers, and boyfriends. Private Warren walked up to Martin, took off his hat and rubbed his close shaved head.

"I can't believe it. We're United States Marines!" The guys all around him cheered and hollered, "Oorah!"

"Hey Davis, we're going to Marco's night club later tonight to celebrate getting out of this place, you wanna come?" Warren asked Martin. Martin watched his mom walking up in his direction.

"No thinks, I don't feel much like it." he replied. Warren came up to him and softly spoke to him so no one else could hear.

"Come on, Davis, you need to forget her. Life goes on, ya know? There are so many girls out there that you can just take your pick." Warren said.

"If you don't move on, it'll eat you up inside. You're a Marine now and you're gonna be a pilot! Girls will be coming after you in hoards. Be strong." Warren started making loud grunting sounds and the members of his platoon joined in. Warren stopped his grunting and put his hand on Martin's shoulder.

"Come on man, 7 o'clock. Marco's. Be there." Warren said and walked away. Martin's mom walked up and gave him a big hug.

"Congratulations! You're a Marine now." She said.

"Come with me. We'll spend the day together. You're not leaving for California for a week. Let me have you all to myself for as long as I can." Martin and his mom drove to downtown Savannah, GA, which was a 45-minute drive. They walked around and looked in all the shops, went to the park, and sat and talked. She was sad that her son was going off to California. She wasn't sure why he wanted to go back there. Maybe it was to recapture some old memories of the places he and his father went together, she wondered. They sat down on a park bench in the square and they talked.

"Martin, I'm kind of wondering why you requested to be assigned to Camp Pendleton. Is it because of your old friends and your father's memories?" she asked him. He took a sip of the soda he held in his hand and thought of what to say.

"Well, not exactly." he answered. He took another drink from his soda and remained quiet for another moment. Teresa had a look of wonder on her face until it hit her. She understood. It was Diana. He wanted to be near her.

"Oh, I think I understand!" she said, "Do you love her?" she asked with a half smile. He looked up in surprise that his mother had understood what he was not able to say before. A small smile came across his lips.

"Yeah Mom, I do." he said.

"Well, have you told her how you feel?" He looked down at his feet.

"No, not when I had the chance." He had many chances before, he just was afraid to say anything. Martin looked up at the horizon. The sun was beginning to set.

"What does it matter? She's getting married. She wants me to walk her down the aisle. How am I supposed to walk her to another man to exchange vows? How am I supposed to act when I see her in her wedding gown and know it's not me she's wanting to spend the rest of her life with? Mom, how am I supposed to keep quiet when the preacher asks if anyone objects? This feeling I have for her is a curse. One I'll have to live the rest of my life with and there's nothing I can do about it." He did all he could to keep from breaking down. Teresa put her arm around her son.

"Martin. I think that if you love someone enough and show it, you just never know how things will turn out in the end. It really all depends on fate. We're all just pieces in this game of life. God is the player. It doesn't matter what choices we make in life, how we move around. He's the one that will pick us up and move us to where he wants us to be. We don't get to pick who we love or where we fit into their lives. Just be glad that in this short moment we have on earth that we knew them when we did and that wherever they are in their life, somewhere, sometime even if it's many years from now, our love for them will have its moment to shine in their heart. He just looked on as she spoke. She continued.

"Now ask yourself this question. Do you really think that all the love you feel for her is a waste just because she doesn't know about it yet? Well it's not! To have that much love for one person is amazing. To have the opportunity to feel that kind of feeling is a blessing, not a curse. If you think about it, you are giving her the most precious gift by loving her. And I know she would be very grateful for having you love her so much. You let her be who she is for now and just be there for her. That kind of love makes you strong. Love moves mountains. Love gives us the ambition to take on the world, to do things we never would think possible before.

People who love can make miracles happen. Tell me Martin, would you honestly give all that up just to block the pain of not having her love returned?" He looked at her. After a moment of thinking he responded.

"No. No I wouldn't. I knew that from the moment I met her that my life was changed. I'd never give up who I am, what I've become from that strength." She smiled at him proudly.

"That's what I wanted to hear. Now I'll tell you what you need to do. You go to that wedding, and you walk her down the aisle and be there for her. She'll need you. Time and again she'll need you to be there. She won't forget that you were there for her. I guarantee that she won't forget." She looked at her watch and started to stand.

"Now, I better get you back. You have some friends who are waiting to take you out on the town." After they got back, Martin got in his car, waved goodbye to his mom, and drove to Marco's to meet with his buddies on their last night together. When he pulled up in the parking lot, he immediately saw Warren and his friends still in their uniforms, standing by the front door. Warren waved him over. Martin, still in his uniform joined them. Warren, who was smoking a cigarette, threw it down, stomped it out, and put his hand on Martin's shoulder.

"Man, we are gonna do good tonight. There are about 30 single girls inside just waiting for us fresh Marines to dance with them." He saw that Martin didn't look too sure about going to a nightclub and dancing with girls. The only girl Martin wanted to dance with was in California, planning her wedding. Warren lowered his head to Martin's ear and spoke softly.

"Don't think about her man, just come in with us and have a good time, alright?" He wasn't going to let Diana get him down. She was moving on with her life and he needed to too. Martin spoke up with fake enthusiasm. "Her who? The only her I'm interested in is whoever the lucky girl will be tonight! Are we doing this thing or what?"

Warren clapped his hands together, and said to the group of friends, "Well, come on boys, we can't keep these girls waiting." The other guys started whooping and hollering and they hurried inside. Martin followed. Inside, it was dark with only disco lights and black lights glowing. Music was playing loudly. Martin didn't really feel like being there. He didn't feel like meeting girls. All around him were guys and girls dancing. Warren led the group to a table and they all sat down. They looked around them. Warren stood up.

"I'm gonna go get us some drinks." Then he walked away. Martin looked over to a table across the dance floor and saw four girls sitting. One of them was looking at Martin and smiling. She had red hair and looked similar to Diana. He smiled back at her. She turned to one of her friends, whispered and they turned to Martin and smiled at him again. She was wearing a short black skirt and a tight red sweater. A moment later Warren came back with the drinks, set them on the table and sat down. He looked over at Martin and saw him eyeing the girl across the floor, and smiled.

"She's cute. Why don't you ask her to dance?" Warren asked him. Martin took his eyes off the girl and looked back at Warren.

"All in good time my friend. I'm still scoping out options if you know what I mean."

"Well bro, I can tell she likes you. Now be a man and go ask her to dance." Just then the group of girls got up and started walking towards Martin and his friend's table. When they got there, the red head spoke up.

"Hi soldiers, mind of we join you?"

"Not at all." Warren said. He and three of the other boys got up and offered the girls their seats. They thanked them and sat down. When the boys pulled up some chairs and sat down, everyone was quiet for a moment. Warren spoke up first.

"So where are you ladies from?" he asked. One of the girls with short black hair answered.

"From around here. We all go to the local beauty college. I'm LeAnne, and these are my friends; Tina, Becky, and Sharon." she said as she pointed to the red head

"So what's your name soldier?" Sharon asked Martin.

"Uh, Martin." he said with a smile. The fast music stopped and a slow song began to play. Warren and the other boys asked the girls to dance, leaving Martin and Sharon sitting alone. He watched his friends abandon him for the dance floor. Warren glanced over and motioned for Martin to ask Sharon to dance. Martin looked back at Sharon. Putting up a brave front, he took a deep breath and said, "Would you like to dance?" She smiled.

"Yes, I'd like that." They stood up and he walked her to the dance floor. He held her loosely and awkwardly as they began to dance.

"You need to relax." she said, and pulled him closer to her. He was real nervous. He looked over at Warren who was mouthing for Martin to hold her tight and relax. Martin took a deep breath and put his arms tighter around her and held her closer. She put her head down on his shoulder and closed her eyes. Martin looked up at Warren, who gave him the thumbs up. He began to relax a bit. He kept reminding himself that he was single and that he had to move on. He held Sharon closer. She looked up at him.

"So soldier, what are your plans now that you're a Marine?"

"I'm going to go to college, get my degree and go to flight school. I'm going to be a pilot" He explained. She grinned.

"That's awesome!" She gave him a flirty smile. He politely smiled back and hoped the dance would soon end. He wasn't comfortable and in fact, he didn't even want to be at the club. He and Sharon finished the dance and then went to go sit down. She started talking to him about wanting to be a makeup artist and continued to talk about herself. He smiled and pretended to listen. After a while, she asked him if he would drive her to the dorm. He was nervous about going back to her place. He really wasn't ready to jump in to anything. But he knew he had to live his life too. He hunted down his friends to say goodbye. Warren, who was sitting at the table with LeAnne on his lap, was whispering in her ear while she giggled. Warren looked up and said. "Looks like you're back in the game my friend." and gave him a thumbs up.

"Yeah, life goes on, right?" Sharon didn't live very far and when Martin's car pulled up to her dorm, they parked and talked for a minute.

"Do you want to come in?" she asked slyly.

"I don't think LeAnne will be back any time soon." Martin was caught off guard. Normally, he might have taken her up on her offer, but right then, he just couldn't. He knew that Diana belonged to someone else, but he just couldn't be with another girl. It would somehow feel like cheating to him.

"No thanks, I better get going." he said. She looked disappointed but moved closer.

"Well, how about a kiss goodnight?" She leaned in and kissed him. He started to hesitate but kept thinking about Diana kissing Jake and so he let go and started kissing Sharon back. The kiss got deeper and more intense as Diana slipped back into his mind. He suddenly imagined that he was kissing Diana and got lost in the kiss. He closed his eyes and pulled her closer and began to move his hands to her cheek. She moved her mouth down to his neck and started kissing it. He still had his eyes shut and in the heat of the moment let the words slip out in a soft whisper.

"Diana!" She immediately stopped what she was doing and said.

"What? My name is Sharon!" She moved back to the passenger seat and grabbed her purse from the floor.

"I don't normally do this kind of thing you know. I'm not that kind of girl! I thought you were different, Martin! I thought it was me you were kissing like that. I thought you did it because you liked me. But apparently you were thinking of some other girl. Gosh, I was so stupid!" Martin couldn't believe what he was about to do before he had slipped up and said Diana's name.

"I'm sorry, Sharon. I don't think you're that kind of girl. Look, I thought I was ready for this but I was wrong. It's not you at all. It's so complicated." Then she saw the look in his eyes.

"This Diana, she's not here with you tonight, but she's definitely the lucky girl here." Martin looked up at Sharon and gave her a smile. She was right. Diana was the reason he didn't want to go to Sharon's room, and why he had kissed her so passionately. Sharon looked a lot like Diana, but he knew she wasn't her. Sitting in the car with Sharon, he wanted so much for her to be Diana, but she wasn't. Sharon had read right through him. She could see that he had it bad and couldn't replace her with anyone else no matter how hard he tried. Sharon let out a sigh.

"It's just my luck. I meet a good-looking Marine who's going to be a pilot, and his heart's already taken. I sure hope she knows what she's got." she said. They smiled at each other.

"Yeah, well not every story has a happy ending, right?" he said to her. He reached out his hand to her. She took his hand in hers and shook it.

"It was nice meeting you, Sharon," he said.

"It was nice meeting you too, Martin. You're one of the good ones!" She smiled, opened her car door and climbed out.

"And if it doesn't work out between you and this girl, look me up." she said as she closed her door. He watched her walk away, then he reached into his glove box and pulled out the last letter he had gotten from Diana. He wasn't going to wait for fate to step in. He made up his mind that he was going to tell her how he felt and stop the wedding. He loved her and he needed to tell her that before she made the biggest mistake of her life. Even if it turned out to be the biggest mistake of his.

The food in first class was much better than Martin thought it would be. The flight attendant had noticedhim wearing his dress blues and upgraded his ticket from coach. He politely turned it down at first, but she insisted. He was on a flight to New York heading to Diana's wedding so he could walk her down the aisle. Only his intentions weren't to do anything more than to tell her how he felt before she got married to this Jake guy. He finished his meal just in time for the flight attendant to walk up. She was a very attractive girl who took notice of Martin right away. When she didn't think he was looking, she would look at him and was giving him lots of attention.

"Would you like me to take your trey sir?" She asked with a smile.

"Yes please." He handed it to her. She took it and put it on her cart before turning back to him.

"Is there anything else I can do for you?" She gave him a flirty smile. He was flattered by her attention.

"No ma'am. I think I'm fine, thank you."

"I'll say!" she said under her breath as she turned away. He smiled as he heard her. Across the aisle Martin noticed an elderly couple. The lady smiled when she saw Martin look over and she spoke up.

"Where are you heading young man?"

"Manhattan, ma'am. To a wedding."

"Yours?" she asked. His lip drew up a small smile.

"No ma'am. Actually I'm just going to see an old friend." "A girl?" she asked.

"I'm right aren't I? I can tell about these things. I'm good at reading people, aren't I Harry?" she asked her male companion sitting next to her.

"That's right! She knew when she first saw me forty years ago that we were meant to be." Harry said.

"Oh so how long have you been married?" Martin asked.

"Five wonderful years!" she said as she looked at Harry and held his hand. Martin was a bit confused.

"Just five years? But didn't you just say you got together 40 years ago?" Harry chuckled.

"No son, we met forty years ago in LA when we both were in college, but my Beth here was engaged to Chris Harrington. Oh but I didn't care. I knew she was the one." Martin leaned in. "But didn't that bother you that you loved her but she was marrying another man?"

"Oh it bothered me alright. I wanted to punch out that Chris Harrington and run away with Beth. But Chris could give her such a better life than I could have. He came from a wealthy family. I was young and poor and didn't have anything to offer her."

"So what did you do?" Martin was intrigued and wanted to know more.

"The only thing I could do. I moved to New York, went to medical school and became a doctor. I was going to do everything I could to make enough money so when she came to her senses and left Chris I would be ready." Harry let out a little giggle.

"And he was right!" Beth interrupted.

"I realized that Chris wasn't the one for me and that I should have followed my heart, and that was my Harry." Beth and Harry looked at each other and smiled. Martin interrupted their moment. "I'm still confused. Why did it take so long for you to marry each other?" Harry spoke up. "Well, after I finished med school and got settled into my practice, I got word that she had divorced Chris and so I moved my practice back to LA to win her back. Little did I know that Beth had moved to New York to find me." Beth spoke up.

"I tried to find him by going to every doctor's office I could for years but no luck."

"Meanwhile, I was trying to find her." Harry said. Martin spoke up.

"So how did you finally find each other?" Beth answered first.

"I eventually moved back to LA after my father had passed to be close to my mother. One night driving back from my friend's house my car blew a tire and I ended up driving into some bushes. I hit my head on the steering wheel and was taken to the local ER. As it turns out the doctor on duty was none other than my Harry." Martin smiled. "So you finally got married." Harry and Beth laughed.

"Not quite. You see, Harry was married to Cindy Watson, a nurse he was working with." Harry spoke up.

"I had to live my life. Since I hadn't been able to find Beth all those years, I needed to try and move on." Beth then spoke.

"I couldn't blame him. He was lonely and needed someone there for him. Although I understood, I was heartbroken. I didn't think we would ever get together. I felt I had lost my chance. Being depressed that I had lost him, I wasn't going to hang around. I needed to distract myself from my pain so I decided to join the Peace Corp. For ten years I traveled all over the world helping out people less fortunate than myself. I watched people around me fall in love and get married. I even was proposed to a few times by a couple of men in the Peace Corp, but my heart was already taken. It wasn't right to accept anyone's proposal when I couldn't give them all my heart." Martin was getting anxious.

"So what happened then?" Harry spoke up.

"After five years of being married to Cindy, it ended. She knew she couldn't really replace Beth, so she moved on. That same year I needed to just get away and so I closed up my practice and moved to Africa where I could help sick people there who really needed medical care. One day, after I'd been over there for five years, I saw a woman walk into my hut asking for medicine for some sick children in a village nearby. As soon as I saw her face, I thought I had died and gone to heaven. It was my Beth." Beth smiled and said.

"We were both finally single at the same time! We got married a week later. We didn't want to waste any time. We wanted to grab the other before they got away again. We've been together every second since." Martin smiled at them both.

"That's the most amazing story I've ever heard! I'm so glad you finally found the happiness you both were destined to have." Beth spoke up. "You see son, life don't always work out the way you plan. But if you stay true to your feelings and never give up your dreams, anything can happen. You never know. She may feel the same way about you and maybe she just needs to know how you really feel first." Harry added.

"Don't give up on this girl. If she's the one and you know it, don't let go." Just then the captain came on over the intercom, announcing they would be landing in Queens in just a few minutes. Martin sat back in his seat. He was in awe. This couple had met and fell in love forty years ago and even though they had married other people, they were meant to be together and against all odds, fate made sure that happened. He wanted in his heart to believe that he and Diana were destined for that kind of fate. That even though their lives are in different directions, one day they will be together and as happy as Harry and Beth.

Martin was unpacking his suitcase in his hotel room. It had been a long flight and he was tired but the wedding was in two hours. It was being held in the main ballroom of the hotel. He knew she must be there somewhere, or would be soon. He was nervous to see her, but excited. He kept thinking about Beth and Harry. It must have been hard on them to be so in love but see the other married to another person. He would have thought that when you lose your chance, that it's gone forever. But they proved him wrong. He sat down at the desk with a pen and piece of paper. He was going to write her about how he felt. He was going to give it to her to read before the wedding. He knew he was taking a giant risk and had no idea how it would end up, but he needed to say how he felt and tell her once and for all.

Dear Diana, This may come to you as a surprise but I want you to know the truth. I lied to you that night in the tree house. When you asked me if I had said I love you. I did, and I do. From the moment I first met you and through all these years that we have been apart it's always been you. You remember the night we both made wishes on a shooting star?

Well my wish was that we would end up together. Please don't marry Jake. Marry me. Be with me. I can give you all the happiness you deserve. I want you to know that no matter what I see or do that there is nothing in this world that I want more than to fall asleep with you in my arms each night and to wake you with a kiss each morning. I want it to be me that you have children with. I want to see them grow up with you by my side. Every day I am trained to fight. I've learned that anything that makes you happy is worth fighting for. But there is nothing in this world to me that's worth fighting for more than you. There is nothing that even compares to you. I didn't have to go around the world to find out where my happiness was when it was right next door. With All My Love, Martin.

He folded the letter up and put it in an envelope. He wrote on the front of the envelope.

"For Diana, please read before you marry Jake." Martin walked down to the lobby to have his letter delivered as quickly as possible to her room. He walked up to the front desk and waited for the lady behind the counter to help him. As he stood there waiting for her to finish helping an older man, he overheard three young women behind him in a conversation. He could tell by what they were saying that they were there for Diana's wedding. One girl was talking.

"I am so excited for Diana. I can't believe she is finally marrying Jake. He is so dreamy."

"Yes he is." another girl added.

"She is so lucky! He has lots of money and she won't ever have to go without. He's paying for her to go to college you know. And with his connections he pulls strings and gets her auditions too." The first girl said again.

"I know. She was just saying to me this morning how lucky she is to be marrying him. She is so in love." The third girl spoke up.

"Come on you two, we need to go get our bridesmaids dresses on." And with that the girls walked away.

Martin had heard everything they had said about Diana being so in love with Jake and so happy. What kind of friend would he be if he tried to interfere and break them up? She would probably hate him for ruining her chance at happiness. He wanted her, wanted to let her know how he felt so she would chose him, but not at this cost. The lady at the counter walked up to him.

"Sir, would you like me to deliver that for you?" She held out her hand waiting for him to hand the letter to her. He stood for a moment looking at the envelope he held in his hand. Finally he spoke.

"No thanks!" he said and walked over to a trash can. He paused for a moment and just looked at the letter before he dropped it in. The ballroom the ceremony was in was decorated beautifully with lots of ribbons and pink rose bouquets. Lace curtains were draped throughout the room making it look like a royal wedding. Guests were just about done shuffling in and finding seats. Diana was standing out in the hall by the ballroom. She was there with her best friend and maid of honor Katherine, and two bridesmaids in pink dresses. She kept looking around for Martin. She wasn't sure if he was going to show up and walk her down the aisle. He was late. Suddenly the music started, which was her signal to start descending down the aisle. She was busy straightening her veil and the train to her gown when she heard Katherine.

"Oh my God! What a babe! Check out the hot soldier boy in the suit." Diana looked over to where Katherine was pointing and then she saw him. Martin. For a moment they both stood still just looking at each other, not looking away. She hadn't seen him for years and here he was, standing there all grown up, and the most handsome guy she had ever seen in his Marine dress blues. She couldn't speak. She couldn't move. He had a small grin on his face as he looked at her in her wedding gown. Never had he ever imagined her looking as lovely as she did that moment in her gown. Finally she spoke up. "You came!" He answered her.

"You asked." After a moment she was pushed by one of the bridesmaids.

"You hear that music? That means you need to walk down the aisle now. Go." She started walking toward him slowly, never taking her eyes off his. He held out his arm and she took it.

"You're beautiful!" He said in a low voice. She smiled big.

"So are you!" He smiled and softly chuckled.

Slowly they turned and walked down the aisle toward where Jake and the minister were waiting. Both of them were walking slower than they needed to because neither of them wanted that moment to end. She turned her gaze around the room to Jake who was waiting with a big grin on his face. She tried not to look at Martin but she couldn't resist and stole glances at him. Her glances were met by his.

Martin knew that he was walking her down the aisle to her awaiting soon-to-be husband, but in his mind he imagined that they were walking together down the aisle to get married. He was fighting his emotions. It was the longest walk of his life, and the shortest. Before he was ready for it to be over, they were at the altar.

They exchanged one last glance and then Martin walked to his seat in the front pew. Diana took Jake's hand and smiled at him. The minister began the ceremony. As he did, Martin sat with his eyes on Diana. His mind was drifting off to the dance they shared that night years ago. She had felt wonderful in his arms. In his heart they're still sharing that dance. He heard the minister.

"If anyone feels that this man and woman should not be wed, speak now or forever hold your peace." Diana turned to Martin, almost waiting for him to say something. Inside he was screaming, "I do! She belongs with me!" But it took every ounce of strength he had to hold his peace inside. After a pause, the minister continued the ceremony. Martin fought back his anger and hurt as he witnessed Diana and Jake exchange vows and rings, and when it was time for Jake to kiss his bride, Martin just looked down. Before he knew it, it was over and the minister was announcing them as Mr. and Mrs. Jake Stein. It was final. She belonged to Jake.

The reception hall was filled with flowers, guests and food. Music was being played while couples danced on the dance floor. Diana and Jake were walking around socializing with their guests. Meanwhile, Martin was sitting at a table with a drink, watching the newlyweds walk around. Diana kept looking over at Martin. She was trying to make her way over to him but kept being interrupted by guests giving their blessings. Martin did his part. He had come to walk her down the aisle, and he didn't interfere in their wedding. He made an appearance at the reception, but was ready to leave. He was torn up inside and needed to go. He waited for her to come to his table but just before she could, Jake announced that he and his new bride were leaving for their honeymoon.

Everyone quickly shuffled out the door and stood by the awaiting limo outside. She quickly threw her bouquet to the girls waiting behind her. After a struggle, an elderly lady ended up with it and held it up with a big smile. Everyone was laughing. Diana was looking all around for Martin but couldn't find him. She didn't want to leave without saying goodbye to him. Jake kept pulling her so she had to give up her search. As she and Jake were making their way to the limo, she was getting lost in the crowd. Suddenly someone pulled her aside. It was Martin. For a moment they just looked at each other. Then suddenly she threw her arms around him.

"Thank you." she whispered to him. They held on to each other for what felt like forever. Neither could let go. But just as suddenly, she pulled away, and before he knew it, she was gone. A moment later, the limo pulled away. Everyone was waiving to the newlyweds as they rode away. Soon the crowd around Martin thinned out until only he was left standing, watching Diana leave him again.

September 5th, 1984

Dear Diana, I'm stationed at Camp Pendleton now. It feels weird being back here. I haven't gone to see my dad's grave yet. I'm not ready for that. It feels so weird being here without Mom. I'm attending college. I have to have a bachelor's degree before I can become a pilot so I have a long road ahead. So how is the Performing Arts School coming along?

Have you met any famous people yet? I would like to come visit you but don't have a minute to myself with my training. I sold my car before I moved, so right now, I have no transportation. I have to catch a bus around base. I would like to see you. Please send me your new address. I tried to find you in the phone book, but there is no listing.

I know you have moved since you got married because I went to that address when I first got here, but your mother had moved to New York and you moved out. The new homeowners gave me your P.O. box number. I know you are somewhere in LA. Please write me when you get this letter so I know where you are. With love, Martin. He waited for her to respond to his letter, but it came back.

"Return to Sender; No Such Person." was written on the front. Within five years, he sent fifteen letters that were never answered. He had no more leads on her and even tried to find out from James where she was but he hadn't heard from her either. Martin had just about given up, but still held hope that someday soon he would find her. Martin graduated college, finished flight training and was officially a fighter pilot. It was December of 1989 and Martin had been serving a six month tour of duty on an aircraft carrier off the coast of Japan. The soldiers were getting a treat as a USO tour was on board to perform for them. It was a surprise Christmas performance for the soldiers away from their families over the holidays. Captain Martin Davis and Captain Oliver Warren sat in the 5th row as the show began. Two men who did a comedy act were first and left the audience in stitches. Second was a magic trick performed by a celebrity that Martin had seen on TV. He was enjoying himself. The crowd loved it. Any type of entertainment on the ship was a welcome for the soldiers. The Announcer came on.

"That was The Amazing Alfred." he said.

"And now for our next number. She's a beauty all the way from Cali. The wonderful singing voice of Mrs. Diana Stein." Martin's heart stopped. The crowd began to applaud. The place grew dim and the crowd watched as a female figure emerged from behind the curtain. All around Martin, men were whistling when they saw her.

His Diana was standing on stage. She had her beautiful auburn hair in curls, wearing a red sequenced dress. She looked more beautiful than Martin had ever imagined. She had grown into quite a beautiful woman. Nothing like the T-shirt and cut off jean shorts he had seen her wear. His eyes were glued to her. He didn't move, he couldn't breathe. She was there! Of all places to see her, it was here on an aircraft carrier out at sea, half a world away from where he lived. Music began to play. She started singing. There was a hush as she began. The song was one he knew. It was a Christmas song of being away from home at Christmas time. It was sad but beautiful.

Martin sat there, watching her. Soaking up her presence. It had been over six years since he last saw her. But as she stood there on stage singing, he felt just as much love for her as he had six years earlier.

"That's her! That's Diana!" Martin softly said to his buddy.

"The girl you write to is Diana Stein? Man, you didn't tell me that! Lucky dog, you! No wonder you can't get over her." Martin nudged him.

"Cut it out!" They both chuckled. All around Martin and Warren, tough Marines were tearing up as she sang to them, making them think of their families left behind back at home. He could hear their sobbing. He couldn't take his eyes off her, and he didn't want her to stop singing. But she did. She finished her song and smiled and waved as the crowd gave her a standing ovation. She blew the crowd a kiss and walked back stage behind the curtain.

"I'll be right back, man." Martin said softly.

"Hey! See if you can get me an autograph!" Martin got up out of his seat and walked towards the back stage entrance. The announcer came on over the intercom. "Let's hear it for the very lovely and talented

Mrs. Diana Stein. Now for our last act. The dancing Richardson sisters." Martin wasn't paying attention to who was coming out on stage. Since no one was paying him any attention due to the performance, he opened the door, and walked in. Inside, people were scurrying about getting ready to perform. He looked around and couldn't see her at first. Then as a group of girls moved away, there she was with her back turned towards him. She was hanging up an outfit. He wanted to put his arms around her but thought better of it. Just then Martin was stopped by a guard.

"Hey, you can't be back here Captain Davis"

"I know her! I want to talk to Diana." Diana heard his voice and stopped moving. She turned around and when she saw him, her face lit up.

"Martin, is that you?" she asked as she looked him over. He smiled.

"Oh my God! I can't believe it's you!" she screamed. She threw her arms around him. He lifted her up, swung her around and they danced in an embrace for a moment. He didn't want to let go. She felt so wonderful in his arms. He had waited so long to see her; he felt like he was dreaming! He put her down and she looked him over.

"Wow, look at you! Captain Davis!", she said as she read his name tag.

"You did it! You're a pilot now!" she said excitedly.

"Why haven't you written me?" she asked as she playfully punched him in the arm.

"I thought you had forgotten about me."

"No way!" he answered.

"You moved and I couldn't find you." he explained. Her smile faded. She got a funny look on her face. I wrote you with my new address. I asked Jake to send it to you. I guess it got lost in the mail. She walked over to her purse, which was sitting on the counter beside her.

"Here, I'll write it down along with my phone number." She wrote her information down on the back of a photo of herself and handed it to him.

"Please don't lose it."

"I'll guard it with my life." he said as he held the picture to his heart. Just then, Jake came up behind Diana, grabbed her arm and swung her around.

"Come on babe, we need to get ready. As soon as this last act is over, we need to be at the helicopter to fly out. We need to be packed and ready to go in, like ten minutes!"

"Wait," Diana told him.

"Jake, you remember Martin." Jake held out his hand and he and Martin shook.

"Martin!" Jake said.

"Martin is a pilot now, isn't that great!"

"Keeping our airways safe, huh?" Jake asked him.

"I do what needs to get done." Martin said back.

"Well I'm sure Diana and I can sleep better at night." Jake said with a smile and a bit of sarcasm. He gave Diana a look and walked off.

"Nine minutes!" he called back to her. She looked at Jake, rolled her eyes and looked back at Martin.

"Look, I have to get all packed. We're heading to Italy right after the show. Listen, you take care of yourself up there. Alright?" she asked him with a serious look on her face.

"I will." he said.

"Promise me you will, okay? I mean it! You stay safe!" She kissed his cheek.

"You have my word, Milady!", he told her. She smiled, leaned over and kissed his cheek again. She started walking towards a storage room. She turned around and yelled, "Don't forget to write me okay? Your letters, they mean a lot!" Then she disappeared around a corner, and he watched her walk away again.

Chapter Nine

January 6, 1990

Dear Diana, It was wonderful seeing you. I was taken by surprise. I thought your performance was terrific. I hope you're doing well. We are so busy here and I hardly have time to think, much less write. I am sorry this letter is so short. We're going home soon. Everyone is so excited. I will write you again when I can. I just wanted to say hi. Take care! Love, Martin January 20, 1990 Dear Martin, I am so glad to hear that you are doing fine. I have great news. I didn't get to tell you this when I saw you, but I've got a recording contract. Isn't that wonderful? I thought it would never happen. I was performing at a benefit months ago when a record producer, Larry, heard me singing. He loved my voice.

A week later, I was signed on with a big label. Me! I can't believe it. Both our dreams came true! You are a pilot and I'm a recording artist. I've got a song you may be hearing on the radio any day now. It's all so exciting and I feel like I'm going to wake up and it all be just a dream. I just wanted to tell you the good news. Please be careful over there. I worry about you, you know.

Take care, Love,

Diana

February 10, 1990

Dear Diana,

I am so proud of you! You did it!! That's great! I bet your album will be a #1 hit. Wait and see. I will be watching for you at the Music Awards. I only have a minute to write. My schedule is so packed. I hardly have time to breathe. Please write soon!

Love,

Martin

P.S. I still have one more dream to work on.

October 19, 1990

Dear Diana,

I have been following your career and I know that you are doing very well and are making a name for yourself. I cut out all the newspaper articles I come across on you and have kept them in a scrapbook. I have tried to call you at the phone number you gave me but I keep getting your answering service. You're a hard person to get hold of. I guess being in the recording studio takes up most of your time.

As you know, there is stuff happening in the Middle East and they are sending in troops to rectify the situation. I'm on the list to be sent out next week. I'm not looking forward to it, really, but I'm a Marine now, and I have to play my part. This is what I have been trained for. I have to be ready to try and save the world. I will write you while I'm over there, but mail can take about a month to be cycled through, so my news from the front probably won't be news to you by the time you hear it from me.

Mom is worried out of her mind that her little boy is being sent off to a war zone. I know it breaks her heart. But she can't help being scared to lose me too. I miss you. I hope you are doing fine. I can't wait to see you again. I want to take you up for a ride in a plane like I promised you. I'll write soon. All my love, Martin Diana's heart fell as she read that he was being sent to war. A tear ran down her cheek as she folded up the paper and put it back in the envelope.

"What are you going on about now?" Jake asked from across the room. He had been watching a football game and drinking a beer when he was interrupted by her sobs.

"Martin is being sent off to Desert Storm. They're sending him to war!" she said.

"So what." said Jake.

"Isn't that why he joined in the first place? To be a war hero or something. We'll see just how brave he really is." Jake said with sarcasm. He had been drinking quite a bit and was quite inebriated. Diana walked over to Jake, pushed him on the arm.

"Stop being a jerk." Just then, Jake jumped up, grabbed her by the arm and held it behind her back.

"Don't you ever call me a jerk!" he said angrily.

"Do you understand me?" he yelled at her. She couldn't talk. She was in so much pain and shock by his actions that she didn't know what to say.

"You act like you have feelings for him. You remember that it's me who you're married to. Not him. Who put you through school? Who helped you get that recording deal, huh?" he growled. Not pretty boy in a Marine uniform playing toy soldier; me!"

"Let go, Jake, you're hurting me." she cried out, but he didn't let go. The circulation in her arm was beginning to be cut off.

"Who made you what you are now? If it weren't for me, you'd still be plain Diana Taylor, living as a waitress to pay your way through school. You just remember that!" he yelled. He let go of her arm, grabbed the letter from her hand, tore it up and walked over to a bookshelf and pulled out an old cigar box and pulled out a bunch of opened envelopes.

"Here are his letters to you. Just a friend huh? Doesn't sound like it to me by how he writes to you. All my love, Martin. She looked at the stack of letters he was holding with surprise.

"His letters, you were hiding them all these years? How could you?"

"Because you are my wife and I won't have some fly-boy trying to make the moves on my girl! He's a fool, and apparently I've been one too!" Jake threw the stack of letters at her and stormed out of the apartment. She fell to the floor, sobbing. She looked down at the pieces of Martin's ripped letter and picked up a small piece with "All my love, Martin." written on it.

She held it to her chest. Jake wasn't the same man she fell in love with. He was a monster. She tried calming herself down. He must have been in an extremely bad mood, she thought. He'll never treat her like that again. Diana spent every alone moment she had reading through Martin's missing letters. She felt like they were all she had of the happy days from her past; before her life had turned mad. Martin's Aircraft Carrier was positioned about 12 miles off of

Kuwait in the middle of the day. He was on his way to chow. His nerves were shot to be so close to the war. He was in it now, not just hearing about it on the news. He didn't feel like eating, but he had to keep up his strength for the upcoming mission.

Once inside the mess hall, he stood in line and got his food. As he walked towards the tables to sit, he saw Captain Warren, Major Smith and Major Green signaling him to sit with them. He nodded to let them know he saw them and walked towards them. He sat his tray down by Major Smith and sat down next to him. "Hey Davis, how's it going?" Major Smith asked him.

"Well, not bad considering where we are." he answered.

"Ah you got that right, man." Capt. Warren said, as he took a drink. After Martin took a bite of his alleged Salisbury Steak, he spoke up.

"So what have you heard?" He asked.

"Well, seems that

"So-damn-insane" isn't listening to our threats, so from what I hear, February 24th is the day we come knocking on his door."

"Man I gotta be honest. I don't even want to think about if anyone will be near where we drop um'. I didn't want to kill anyone. I just wanted to be a Marine, and be all I can be!" Capt. Warren joked. Major Green elbowed him.

"Man, that's the Army. We're the few, the proud!" Major Green said with pride.

"Yeah, well, if we don't all do our job, we might be the few." Capt. Warren said.

"Man, don't say that. That's bad karma." Capt. Smith said.

"Just what we don't need." Martin chuckled at his friends. They ate and talked about the days ahead. Outside, jets were flying over loudly and startled them for a moment. They were scared to be there, and even more scared at the thought that they were going to be dropping bombs in a few days. They all had gone through the combat training, but were not prepared for the real thing. Shooting dummies and props was one thing. Killing real people was quite another.

Diana kept her eyes glued to the TV whenever the news was on with any information about the war.

The bombing had begun. She was worried about Martin. She couldn't help it. He was her best friend. She had to sneak and watch the news when Jake wasn't around; otherwise, he would get mad and turn the TV off in a rage. She had to write him. She knew her letter wouldn't make it there for probably a month, but she knew he would want to hear from her. She could guess that he really needed a friend. He had been there for her, and she wanted to be there for him. She picked up a pen and paper and began to write him.

January 4th, 1991

Dear Martin,

I know you won't get this letter for a while, but I want you to know that I'm thinking about you and my prayers are with you. I watch the news every chance I get and hope that I don't hear that you have been hurt. Your mother called me today. She wanted to know if I had heard anything from you. I guess I won't for a while. Dad isn't really ready to talk to me yet. He never got used to the idea that I was with Jake. Are they feeding you well?

I hope you get well rested there, but probably not, huh? It saddens me that it had to come to this! Now we can only hope for quick peace. I hope the President knows what he's doing. I miss you. People here are wearing yellow ribbons to show their support to our wonderful troops. I wear one too. People tie them to their cars, around trees, and tie them to their fences. Our church even had a midnight prayer service. I am anxious to hear from you and to know that you are okay. Please write as soon as you can.

With love,

Diana

February 24th 1991

Martin and his buddies stood on the flight deck of the aircraft carrier by their jets.

"Well, Boys, this is it." Smith said.

"The moment we've all been trained for." Martin saluted his two buddies.

"Gentlemen, whatever happens, it's been a pleasure serving with you." The four of them stood saluting each other in a moment of silence.

"Now let's go up and kick some butt." They all let out grunts and howls, patted each other on the back, and went to climb in their jets. Martin climbed into the front seat of the jet and Warren climbed in the back. As they were getting ready for their flight, Martin took out Diana's picture from underneath his flight suit, looked at it for comfort and inspiration, then put it back. He was nervous about the fight and what was to come ahead. They were to drop fire on an empty warehouse used for storing weapons. Marin and Warren both looked over at Smith and Green, whose jet was next to theirs and gave them thumbs up. They looked up at them and smiled and returned the gesture. They all got strapped in their seats and put on their helmets.

"Hey Warren, are you all set?" Martin asked him.

"All ready to roll!" he answered back. There was a microphone and a tiny speaker in the helmets so they could talk to each other.

"Smith, Green, how about you two? Are you ready to roll?" Martin asked him.

"All ready to rock n'roll!" he answered and gave them both a wave. Smith's jet was in front of Martin and Warren's jet. They watched as the other jet was launched off the flight deck where they then flew off. Then Martin got the clearance to take off. They were launched forward at high speed and within seconds, they were up in the air. Soon they were flying beside Smith and Green's jet. After flying for about 25 minutes, they were close to their bombing area.

"Okay, boys, we're almost to the target. Get ready for your run." Smith said over the COM.

"Roger." Martin replied. Martin looked down at his screen and watched as he approached the target area. Just then, Green came back over the COM.

"Bogies at six o'clock!" Martin turned around and saw two enemy jets behind them. He quickly pulled up on the controls and moved up so he was no longer in the enemy's path. One of the jets fired at Smith's jet, but missed.

"Son of a bitch! I know you didn't just fire at me!" Smith called out. He pulled up on the controls and followed the enemy jet. Smith came around behind him and fired his cannon. The enemy jet burst into flames and went plummeting straight towards the ground, exploding on contact.

"Yaa-hoo!" Smith yelled.

"You don't mess with the best!" said Green.

"Don't get too cocky, there's still another one out there!" Martin quickly pointed out. The remaining enemy fighter was coming up fast behind Martin. Smith yelled, "He's on your tail, pull up." Martin pulled up on the controls just as the enemy fired. Rounds whizzed by his jet, barely missing.

"Man, that was close!" Warren said. Martin reduced speed and fell back to let the enemy get in front of him. As they were passing each other, Martin looked over and for a brief moment, saw the head of the enemy pilot. He suddenly was hit by a feeling of compassion for the man who had just shot at him. Martin knew this was a kill or be killed situation, and he had been trained for this very moment, but with it staring him right in the face, he was afraid. The enemy was in firing range right in front of him. Martin put his finger on the trigger to fire. For a moment, he hesitated. Could he do it? Could he kill? Just then the enemy jet moved out of Martin's firing range.

"Damn!" Martin let out. The enemy jet moved behind Martin and fired. Martin quickly pulled his jet up and over, out of enemy fire. Smith took off after him. He pulled up beside the enemy and gave him the finger. He then moved over behind him and as soon as the enemy was in range, Smith fired. The enemy jet was annihilated.

"Like I said before, don't mess with the Best!" Smith yelled. Just then, a third enemy jet came out of nowhere.

"Ah, Major Smith, I hate to interrupt your victory dance, but it seems they have a friend, who wants to cut in, coming up at five o'clock!" Martin warned. Smith looked behind him and said,

"Alright, let's dance!"

"No, Wait! This one is mine!" interrupted Martin. He pulled up behind the enemy, and when he was in range, Martin put his finger on the trigger to fire. Again, he hesitated.

"Come on Davis, fire!" Warren said from the back. Martin started shaking. He took a deep breath. Smith suddenly moved into the enemy target range.

"Shoot him!" Smith ordered. Martin closed his eyes and pulled the trigger just in time, hitting the enemy aircraft. Martin, Warren and Smith watched as the enemy jet burst into flames and fell out of the sky. Smith let out a big sigh. He and Warren began cheering for Martin, who was silent.

"Oh, my hero!" Smith joked.

"Good work Davis, now let's go hit the target." Smith continued. As Martin turned the jet around, a beeping sound came on all around. The jet started to lose fuel. There was a huge leak coming from the fuel tank. The fuel was pouring out fast.

"Major Smith, we have a problem here. We're losing fuel, and we're losing it fast. We've been hit. The fuel line is damaged." Beeps were going off and a computer voice was saying,

"Warning, fuel low. Warning, fuel low." over and over.

"Do you have enough fuel to make it back to the carrier?" asked Smith. Martin looked down at his fuel gauge. It was almost completely empty.

"No, we won't make it!" Martin answered. Suddenly, the plane started to pitch as the engines died. Martin quickly took hold of the controls, but it was useless. The plane fell into a nosedive.

"Pull up, pull up!" Warren was yelling from the back seat.

"I'm trying!" Martin yelled back. Faster and faster, their plane was dropping towards the ground.

"We have to eject!" Martin yelled.

"Get ready!" He pulled the lever just in time and they were ejected up out of the plane. Moments later, the plane crashed to the ground. Martin and Warren's parachutes floated them down to the ground about half a mile up from the crash site, right into enemy lines. When Martin hit the ground, he hit hard, twisting his ankle and breaking his arm. Shortly after, Warren hit the ground. He hit even harder than Martin. They had landed in a remote area next to a mostly dry riverbed. Martin quickly looked around for any sign of the enemy. They were alone. Martin undid his chute with his good arm and limped over to his buddy. When he reached him, he noticed that he wasn't moving. Martin put his face up to Warren's nose and found that he was breathing.

"Warren, wake up, man." he said. No movement. Warren's helmet was broken. He must have hit something as they ejected or he could have hit his head as he came down to the ground. Martin knew better than to move him in case his neck was broken. Martin took off his helmet and threw it off to the side. He noticed blood on the side of Warren's head. He took out his pocket knife. Even though it was difficult to do one-handed, he cut a ribbon out of Warren's parachute using his good hand and his teeth, and made himself a sling for his arm, and put it on. The sun was beating down on the two of them and he knew that they both would burn up being exposed to the sun as they were, not to mention they were sitting ducks. They needed cover. Martin decided to make a tent over him and Warren. He took four long branches that he found on the ground, and propped up his parachute with it. He didn't know how long they would be out there, but he knew that Smith wouldn't leave them out there to die.

Martin could tell by the sun's position that it would soon be dark, and he knew that in the desert, even though it's blazing hot in the day, it gets pretty cold at night. He covered Capt. Warren with the remaining parachute for warmth, once it began to get dark. All around them was the sound of enemy fire in the distance. He knew that at any moment, the enemy could come and shoot them both dead. They had no weapons to defend themselves with, except a pocket knife. He kept as quiet as possible. He wanted to make a fire for warmth, but knew better.

The enemy would see the fire and it would bring them right to the two of them. Martin knew that their squadron would be looking for them, but he also knew that with the enemy around, it might take a while before they could get to them. His arm and ankle were killing him and he longed for an aspirin for the pain. He also longed for a hot bath, and a nice warm bed. He longed for food. Even for what they were serving in the mess tent. His stomach was grumbling, but he tried to take his mind off of it. He thought about the poor man he had killed. His fellow officers might have called him a hero, but he felt like a coward because he stalled. He also thought of

Diana. How he missed her. How beautiful she was in her wedding gown. He went to grab her picture from under his flight suit, but it wasn't there. It must have fallen out when he ejected. He longed for her.

Even facing death, she was there in his mind and in his heart. He stayed by his buddy's side the rest of the evening and all through the night, only leaving to relieve himself nearby. Even though Warren remained unconscious, Martin talked to him quite often, telling him that they would be found any minute and that he would be okay, and that they would soon be looking back and laughing at their predicament.

For two days, he watched over his buddy, making sure he was still alive and giving him some water from the small accumulation of rain water in the dry riverbed nearby. He had found a piece of metal on the ground that was curved so he used that to scoop up water to drink and to gave water to Warren every now and then to keep him hydrated. He didn't want to think about what was in that water, but he had no way of filtering it so he had no other choice. Jets were flying over and he could hear the distant sound of explosions. But he kept his vigil by Warren's side. He had no idea if they were going to be found by his squadron before the enemy found them.

Martin was lying down, glancing up at the stars out of the small hole in the makeshift tent he had made. Then he started thinking about Diana again. All around them was the sound of war, but under all the noise, he began to hear a voice singing. It was a beautiful voice that sounded like an angel. He began to wonder if they were dead. He knew that voice. It had been in his dreams for years. It was Diana's voice he heard. He was beginning to hallucinate due to the heat and dehydration. He smiled as he heard the voice singing. He closed his eyes, and just like he did years ago, he drifted off to sleep hearing her angelic voice.

"Capt. Davis, you in there?" He heard a voice outside of the tent. It was morning and someone was walking around outside.

"Diana?" he softly whispered as he held his head up to see who it was. He heard a male voice.

"No, Davis, it's me," Smith replied. Smith peeked his head into the tent where Martin could see him.

"Boy, you must be hallucinating if you think my voice sounded that feminine." Smith said with a smile. Just then, Warren began to move around a bit. He looked around and began to speak.

"Oh, my head hurts like hell! Am I dead?"

"No I think the two of you will pull through." Smith said as he handed a canteen full of water to Martin. He grabbed the canteen with his good arm and took a long drink, and then held it over Warren's mouth so he could drink.

"I'm sorry it took so long for us to get to you." Smith began to explain.

"The enemy was too close to this area. We had to wait for them to leave before we could come get you. We saw this sad little tent in the sand, and knew that it must be you two." he said.

"We better hurry and get the heck out of here before they return." Martin stood up, and helped Smith carry Warren. They each took an arm and carried him out of the tent, and into the helicopter just outside. When they were safely inside, the helicopter lifted off the ground and began their journey back to camp. Smith spoke up.

"Does this belong to any of you? I spotted it about 100 yards from here." He held out Diana's picture. It had a few burnt marks on the corners but Diana's face was not destroyed at all. Martin couldn't believe her picture was saved. He reached for it and took it from Smith. When they were up about three hundred feet, they saw the remains of their jet off in the distance.

"Boy! Lieutenant Colonel Ryan is going to be pissed!" Warren said as he looked down at what was left of their jet. His buddies laughed. Diana was worried. She hadn't heard from Martin and her mind wasn't really on her singing as she was in the recording studio. She would get halfway through the song, but then forget the words. After the fifth time of messing up, Larry came on the intercom.

"Why don't you take a five minute break, Mrs. Stein?" he said. She smiled at him and thanked him. But Jake, who was in the control room, spoke up in anger.

"She can have a break when she gets it right!" He yelled.

"You get your mind off him and onto your job. Pretty boy is where he belongs, trying to save the world. It's costing us big bucks to be in this recording studio. Now you get it right!" She gave him an evil stare and shot back at him. "You don't care about me! You're just in this for the money! The money that I make for you. You're not a husband, you're a moocher!"

"You would be nothing without me, Sweetheart. I did everything for you. I deserve my share now, to get back what I invested in you."

"You've been riding my coat tails from the beginning. Well, not anymore. I'm leaving you!" she yelled. Everyone around them was listening, but she didn't care. She had had it with him. She began to walk away but Jake ran after her and grabbed her arm tightly in his grasp.

"You're not going anywhere until you finish that song!"

"Let go of me you jerk!"

"I told you to never call me that!" Jake raised his hand to slap her but she moved quickly and kneed him right between the legs. Jake let out a gasp and let go of Diana, as he fell to the floor in agony. Everyone around laughed at him. Diana began to walk away but turned back towards him.

"Oh, and since you seem to think that I'm nothing without you, then the microphone's all yours. Cut your own damn song!" And with that, she walked out of the studio, and out of her marriage with Jake.

Chapter Ten

Martin and Warren were shipped straight home. There, they would be treated for their injuries and dehydration. Everyone in his squadron was proud of him. Everyone was proud of him except for himself. He hated having to kill someone. He sank into a depression. He was kept in the infirmary for two weeks. Diana was in LA getting ready to attend a press release of the names of nominees for the Grammy awards when she got a call from Teresa telling her that Martin had been sent back to San Diego. Diana immediately flew in to visit him. She didn't have any trouble getting on base. The guard at the gate recognized her and didn't hesitate to let her in.

"We're pleased to have you here visiting our soldiers, Ms. Stein," the guard told her with a big grin. He told her where to go and she followed the guard's instructions on how to get to the infirmary. She found it with no trouble and pulled her car into the lot and parked. When she walked inside, she saw a front desk with a woman in camo sitting behind it. The lady, still looking down, said, "May I help you?" She looked up and her mouth fell open when she saw Diana. Diana could tell by the look the woman gave her that she had also recognized her.

"I'm here to see Capt. Martin Davis, please." Diana said.

"Just a moment, please," the woman said, trying to hide her excitement at seeing a famous singer. She flipped through some papers and when she found Martin's name, she looked back up.

"He's in room 105. It's right down the hall and to the left." The lady pointed the way.

"Thank you." Diana said with a smile. She began walking away, and noticed that the lady was still looking at her. Diana had gotten somewhat used to being recognized, but not completely. It still took her by surprise at times. She followed the hall and turned left at the corner. She found herself right in front of room 105, and knocked twice. There was a short pause, and then she heard a male voice inside.

"It's open." Diana took a deep breath, and opened the door. Inside, she saw Martin lying in bed with his arm in a sling. He looked like death. He was staring ahead and didn't notice her until she was standing by his bed. His face lit up when he saw her.

"Diana." he whispered. She pulled up a chair and sat down next to him. He lifted up his good arm and put his hand up against her cheek.

"Is it really you?" he asked. He thought he might be hallucinating again. She smiled.

"Yes, it's me, silly." she said.

"You look great." he told her.

"Thanks, you look like hell." she answered with a slight giggle. He turned his head away, smiled and turned back.

"Oh gee, thanks." he told her. She looked at his arm.

"So how are they treating ya here?" she asked.

"Well, I guess I can't complain. I'm missing work, being waited on hand and foot, and getting paid for it." he answered. She was silent for a moment.

"I was nominated for a Grammy." she said. He looked at her and smiled.

"Wow, that's really great." he said but with little enthusiasm. It caught Diana by surprise. She was sure he would have been really happy for her. She looked down to the floor. There was silence. She pushed back her hair and Martin caught a glimpse of a fist size bruise on her cheek.

"What happened?" he asked her, pointing to the bruise. She looked up and ran her fingers along her cheek.

"I fell." she said with half a smile. Martin wasn't falling for it. He knew a bruise from a fist when he saw one.

"Is he hitting you?" Martin asked with anger. Diana looked at him like she didn't know what he was talking about.

"Who?" she asked.

"Jake!" Martin answered back. Diana grew silent and looked down to the floor. She didn't want to answer his question, so she didn't. Martin was growing angry inside.

"That bastard, I'll kill him if he ever hits you again. You tell him that!" Martin yelled at her. She couldn't believe the way he was acting. He wasn't acting like himself. She assumed it had to be due to what he had just been through. She had read somewhere that men who came back from war sometimes weren't in their right state of mind due to the stress of killing and almost being killed. She didn't want to let Martin's actions get to her. She couldn't find anything to say. She looked up at him and he was staring down at his arm.

"I hear they consider you a hero around here." she said with a smile. Martin looked forward at the wall ahead of him.

"Yeah, lucky me! They think I'm such a hero because I killed someone." he said. She frowned.

"They consider you a hero because of the way you took care of your partner!" she answered him. He continued to ramble on, as if he didn't hear her.

"That man, he didn't want to die. I didn't want to do it. I had to follow orders. I'm not a hero, I'm a coward" he said, as if he was talking to himself and not her. He turned to her.

"Did he have a wife? A son? My God Diana! What did I do?" Tears began to well up in his eyes. She felt bad for him.

"You did what you had to do, or you and your partner would have been killed. You're a hero, Martin. If not to yourself, than to your partner, and to me. You saved me once remember? I know how hard it must have been for you," she said, trying to comfort him. He looked over at her and gave her a look that chilled her.

"You don't know. How could you know what it was like?" he asked her with anger. She was confused. She didn't know how to act around him when he was being that way.

"I was just trying to…." He interrupted her again.

"I know what you were trying to do. You were trying to pity me, weren't you?" he snapped at her.

"You were too busy in your penthouse in L.A. with your macho husband who thinks beating on his wife gives him power!" he began to yell. Tears welled up and fell down her cheeks. He was scaring her. She stood up and started walking backwards toward the door. He kept on yelling at her.

"Martin, I came here to tell you that me and Jake…" she began, but he interrupted her.

"Do you love him? Do you love that bastard who beats you?" Martin asked her. When she didn't answer, he continued.

"You don't know real love, Diana. You just don't have a clue. Love isn't being with someone because you're afraid of being alone." She began to yell, his words struck a nerve.

"I'm not afraid of being alone, I…" He interrupted her again.

"True love is your every breath, your every move, what you live for and die for. What keeps you sane at night when you're all alone with nothing else in the world. It's what makes you whole. True love has always been with you, and you choose to ignore it, like you're afraid of it. Don't ignore it anymore!" he said. She was all confused. He wasn't making sense to her.

"I guess you just can't understand and will never get it. So why don't you just go back to your husband who apparently can't keep his hands off you and leave me alone." She was crying and she couldn't understand why he was being so mean to her.

"You bastard!" She replied.

"You have no idea how I feel and how deeply I have loved, or how much I have suffered because of it." She turned and grabbed the doorknob. She turned back around with her face soaked in tears.

"And I guess you'll never know!" She shot at him and turned to walk out the door, slamming it behind her. He felt like he was going to explode inside. He picked up a book off his bedside table, and threw it across the room. He had wanted to shake her and tell her how much he had loved her, that her being with a creep like Jake was a horrible mistake. He had loved her too much and it was killing him inside. She was all he lived and breathed for, she was the one keeping him up at night, and she was also the one making his life miserable. It was right in front of her face the whole time and she couldn't see it.

He was fed up. She was flaunting her happiness in front of him and it was destroying him. He saw how he had made her cry and for a moment, he was content. She was finally feeling the pain she had been putting him through all those years. He wanted to hold her, and he wanted to scream at her all at the same time. Everything he had ever done, all the choices he had made were because of her. He loved her, he hated her. He hated himself even more for treating her the way he did. He wished he were dead. He wished he had died out there in the desert. He already felt dead inside, due to the love Diana had for a husband who abused her and for the love she didn't have for him.

Martin sank even more into a depression after Diana's visit. He just sat staring at the wall in front of him. He felt like the world's biggest fool. The one person he loved more than life, he had just driven away. But he couldn't help how he felt. The more he wanted to reach for her, the more he pushed her away.

And the more she was pushed away, the more he died inside for her. He tried to make himself forget her, forget she even existed. He tried to forget the world around him as well. For five days he didn't say a word, he just sat up in bed, staring out the window across the room. One day, Warren showed up to visit him.

"Hey, Capt. Davis, It's time to get your butt out of this bed. Me and the guys are taking you to the beach!" he said. Martin looked up at him and said, "I don't feel like going anywhere. I'm just not ready." Warren spoke up.

"Come on, you have to get through this. You saved me and Major Smith. You are a war hero!" Martin gave him a sharp glare. "That's bull, and you know it. I'm no hero, I'm a coward. I had a job to do. Tough Marine. I started to wimp out. I almost let Smith and Green get killed." he said as he looked down.

"We all got scared up there. It's totally understandable. You just have to not let it get to you. You have to get past it. And I'm here to help you all the way." Warren said while patting him on the back.

"Now get your lazy butt out of bed, or I'm gonna have to pick you up and haul you over my shoulders like a duffel bag and parade your sorry butt outside!" Martin began to smile.

"Now what do you say?" Martin thought for a moment. He realized he had been feeling sorry for himself too long and that he needed to take back control of his life. Warren was right; it was time for him to get past it, somehow. "I'm getting up." he said.

"Oh, let me run you a shower, you are in terrible need of one my friend." Warren kidded him.
Martin sat on the beach watching his buddies Warren, Smith and Green swimming in the water. They kept yelling for him to join them. Martin just kept staring out at the water. He seemed to be lost in his thoughts and his emotions. He got up, slowly walked toward the shore. He continued to walk into the water with his shoes and clothes on. He was waist deep when Warren looked over from where he was in the water.

At first he thought Martin was coming to join them. But he soon realized that Martin wasn't out there for that reason at all. Martin felt hopeless, defeated and alone. He wasn't thinking clearly. But in the water, he saw for a moment a way out. He stood still and just stared down at the water around him. Warren was calling out to him, but he was ignoring him. Warren moved over to him but before he was able to reach him, Martin went under. Warren yelled for him, then dove into the water. He couldn't find Martin at first. The waves made it hard for him to move. Seaweed was getting in his way. Suddenly, he found Martin and pulled him back up to the surface of the water.

"What the hell are you doing, man?" Warren yelled. He was worried about his friend. Martin finally snapped out of it after a moment.

"Why didn't you let me do it?" Martin was sobbing.

"Do what, huh? Throw everything away? Give up on everything and everyone in your life?"

"What life? I lost my dad, my best friend, and Diana doesn't need me in her life. I'm a failure Warren. I can't pretend anymore that I matter to people. How can I when they keep leaving or turning away?"

"Man, you aren't a failure! You matter to me, you hear me? You're my best friend! I'll never walk away from you, or let you do something crazy or stupid!" Warren assured him. Martin looked at his friend.

"It's over. I've lost. I don't have any more fight left in me. She made her choice! I'm not good enough. I never was! I need to face it." Green and Smith were there, standing by Martin and Warren. They witnessed the whole thing unfold. Smith spoke up.

"You will never be not good enough for anything, man." Green said.

"You can't control your fate any more than the rest of us. We were up there with you, going through it, facing death together. We're sure as hell not going to leave you alone now!" Martin looked up at his friends. They were right! They all had gone through hell too. He realized that even if he didn't have Diana, he had the best damn friends a guy could ever have.

"You guys are the best!" he said to them.

"Yeah, well we are a pretty damn good team!" Warren said. Martin smiled and they all put their arms around each other. He needed them to show him that he'd never be alone with his friends around him. They were his brothers.   Martin returned to work, but he did paper work until his arm fully healed before he could return to flying. He had had time to think about things and he knew he should write Diana and apologize to her. He knew she probably would return his letter, unopened, but he had to try. One day he picked up a piece of paper, and started writing.

February 8th 1991

Dear Diana,

First of all I want to apologize for the way I acted when you came to visit me. The war was hard on me, but that's no excuse for the way I behaved. My arm is healed and I am returning to flying tomorrow. Boy, have I been looking forward to it! This paperwork job they have me doing is driving me nuts. Anyway, they're having a parade next week for all the war heroes of Desert Storm and my Commanding Officer is making me attend. I think the whole thing is crazy.

I just wanted you to know, in case you wanted to come see it or something. I doubt you will come, seeing how I treated you. I can't blame you if you don't come. You probably will throw this letter away, or across the room knowing you. Take care. With love, Martin Diana didn't throw the letter away when she received it, nor did she throw it across the room. Instead, she secretly got on a plane and flew in to see the parade. She didn't let Martin know that she was there in the crowd, wearing dark sunglasses so no one would recognize her.

He looked so handsome in his dress blues. She was proud of him. She wanted to run up to him as his car was driven by during the parade, but this was Martin's moment and she didn't want to be recognized. Martin thought he saw Diana standing in the crowd. He wasn't sure. The woman had on dark sunglasses and seemed to be hiding out in the crowd. But he thought he recognized her red hair. He tried to get a better look from up where he was sitting, but she disappeared behind some people, and was out of view. He thought he was just seeing things. She was taking over his mind. He shook away the thought that it was her. She wouldn't be there watching him, she probably burnt his letter. He was sure she would never talk to him again, after the way he acted.   Martin was back in the air flying and getting his life back together. He had just been promoted to

Major. His best friend, Capt. Warren, was getting married to LeAnne. He asked Martin to be his best man. He was so thrilled to do it. The wedding was beautiful.

Martin stood next to Warren and held the ring for him until it was time to pass it to his buddy. He was happy for his friend. As he watched them dance at the reception, it brought back painful memories for Martin. His best friend was so happy in love, while Martin was so miserable in love. He wanted so much to be dancing out on the floor with Diana in his arms as his new bride. Martin made the wedding toast. He stood up, tapped a spoon on a glass to get everyone's attention.

"Excuse me!" he began.

"Could I have your attention?" When everyone hushed, he continued with his speech.

"When Oliver asked me to be his best man, I was thrilled. I could see how much he was in love with LeAnne. Love is a great and wonderful thing. It's a blessing when the person who you are totally and passionately in love with loves you back just as much." He looked over at his friend and smiled.

"You two have a strong unstoppable love for each other. I envy you, buddy." he said with a smile. Warren smiled and looked at his new bride, who was smiling back at him.

"Let us toast the happy couple! May they always stay as in love as they are right now!" He raised his glass of Champagne up and everyone else did the same.

"To Love." He said "To Love." everyone else repeated. Martin sat down and kept his eyes on the newlyweds. He was happy for his buddy, but he was also envious. Major Smith came over and sat down beside him.

"Hey, I want to thank you for saving me, too." he said as he patted Martin on the back.

"That pilot was about to blow me away when you fired. I know firing was tough on you. Hell, it was hard on all of us. But I know there's more bothering you than just the war. I'm pretty good at guessing people, and my guess is it's a woman. Am I right?" Martin didn't answer. Instead, he looked down, took a drink of his champagne and let out a sigh.

"I knew it." Smith said.

"So what did she do? Break your heart? Did she leave you for another man? Leave you in the dust or something?" Smith asked.

"Something like that." Martin finally replied.

"Hey, let me give you a piece of advice that always works for me when a woman tears me up. Get drunk and forget about her. Find another to take her place. One even better, and soon, you'll forget about the one who broke your heart."

"I've heard that advice before. Besides, it doesn't quite work that way." Martin said, as he took a drink of champagne.

"As far as I'm concerned, there is no one else better, and I'm a cursed man because of it!"

"Wow, you must really have it bad!" Smith said with a surprised expression.

"I guess you're just hopeless."

"Yep, I guess I am." Martin replied as he took the last drink of his champagne. As the reception began to wind down, Martin decided he was too depressed to stay.

"Congratulations, you two." he said to the newlyweds as he approached where they were dancing.

"Thanks." they both told him.

"I'm gonna get going. I've got an early flight tomorrow." Warren frowned.

"Come on, stay a while, there's a girl over there that's been eyeing you all night. Go ask her to dance." Martin wasn't in the mood to dance.

"No, I'm tired. Goodnight." he said.

"Goodnight, man." Warren shook his hand. Martin gave LeAnne a kiss on the cheek and turned and left. When he got back to the barracks, he decided to give his mother a call. He hadn't talked to her in a while and he wanted to let her know that he was okay. He walked over to the pay phone, dropped in his change, and dialed. She answered on the first ring.

"Hello?" She sounded tired.

"Mom, it's me. Did I wake you?" he asked.

"Oh no, it's just been a long day at work. How are you?"

"I'm doing okay." he replied.

"Martin, I'm so sorry I missed your parade. I just couldn't get away. I tried hard, but there was too much going on here with all the wounded soldiers we had returning." she complained.

"That's alright, Mom, I know." They were silent for a moment.

"Diana came to see me a few months ago. Jake's been hitting her. She had a big bruise on her cheek. She was trying to hide it, but I saw it." he told her. Teresa was surprised to hear that was going on.

"James was right about him. I can't believe Diana is with a man like that." she said.

"She deserves so much more. She deserves you, Martin." He smiled. He sure thought so too.

"Mom, I better go. It's late, and we both need our rest. I love you."

"I love you too Son. Keep in touch."

"I will, Bye." He walked back to his room and got in to bed. He was home-sick. He was lonely. He wanted to take back that last moment with Diana and do it right. He wanted to take her in his arms and kiss her. Tell her how much he loved her. He hated himself for the way he had treated her. She had flown in just to see him and he treated her so cold. He couldn't believe how his feelings could make him do things he couldn't seem to control. He wondered about her, what she was doing at that moment. Probably forgiving Jake after he hit her yet again. He reached over and grabbed his dog tags that were hanging by his bed on a hook. His friends had girlfriends who they had given their tags to as a symbol of their affection. He wanted to give his to Diana. He wanted her to be His wife, not Jake's.

He thought about Beth and Harry, the elderly couple on the plane to New York. They were so strong. They waited decades to be together. He wasn't that strong. He wanted her now. He turned the radio on and to his surprise, Diana's latest hit was being played. It was about a love lost. She sounded so beautiful. He lay down and closed his eyes and listened, soaking in every word she sang as if she were singing about him. It got to be too much and he quickly turned it off and threw the little radio across the room.

Chapter Eleven

It was the day before the Grammy Awards in LA. Diana was nominated for best new artist and she was going to sing her new song. She was so nervous that she could hardly think of what to pack to wear. She had been staying in Las Vegas in an apartment with her friend Katherine. When she finally filed for divorce from Jake, she had gone home and packed up her things as fast as she could and hopped a plane. Katherine knew what was going on with Jake and she had offered Diana to come live with her if she ever got the guts to leave him. It was a nice place and she loved being on her own, away from Jake. She was free from his abuse, and it felt great. She picked out a beautiful yellow strapless evening gown from her closet. Yellow was a cheerful color, like the sun, and she was in a cheerful mood.

"So, what do you think of this one for the Music Awards?" she asked Katherine, as she held it up to her.

"Oh, that one looks great on you!" Katherine answered her with a smile.

"Your white pearl necklace and earrings would look stunning with it."

"I'm definitely in the mood for yellow. I feel relieved without Jake, like a weight has been lifted off of me."

"A weight has been lifted off of you, his fist." Katherine said. Katherine gave her a half smile and Diana gave her a shameful look. Just as Diana went to hang the dress on the bathroom door hanger, there was a knock on the front door. Katherine went to answer it. Diana stood looking at the dress. It was her favorite, and she had a feeling it was going to bring her luck at the awards ceremony the next day. Diana heard an argument coming from the other room. Whoever it was at the door, was yelling at Katherine.

"I want to see her!" a voice demanded.

"I know she's here."

"Leave her alone!" Katherine told the man. Diana walked out of the room in time to see Jake push Katherine aside. When she saw him, she stopped in her tracks.

"Jake what are you doing here?" Diana asked him. Jake glared at her. He was in a bad mood.

"You know why I'm here. I'm here to bring you home!" He yelled at her.

"Now get your things and come with me!" he demanded.

"No! I'm not going anywhere with you." she told him.

"I'm not your rag doll to throw around anymore, Jake. Didn't you hear from my attorney? I want a divorce!" He became outraged at what she said. He came towards her. She knew what was coming next, what always came next when they were having a fight. She closed her eyes as he raised his fist in the air and began to bring it down on Diana's face. Just in time, Katherine grabbed his arm from behind him and stopped it.

"You bastard, leave her alone. I won't let you hit her anymore!" She screamed at him. He took his eyes off Diana and turned around to face Katherine. She was still holding onto his arm as hard as she could. He pushed her with all his might and she went flying back and hit her head on the front door and slid to the floor. She was out cold. Diana ran to the back bedroom and slammed the door and locked it. He ran after her. When he tried to open the door and found it was locked, he began to beat on it with his fists.

"Open up, right now! It doesn't have to be like this, just come back with me!" He yelled at her.

"Now open up this door or I'll break it down myself!" Diana remained in the room. She was scared and the first thing that popped in her head was Martin. She needed him. She grabbed the phone that was by her nightstand, went back to the locked door and kept her weight on it. She dialed the number to his squadron office and it rang three times.

"Please pick up." she whispered as tears were streaming down her cheeks. Back at Camp Pendleton, Martin was eating his lunch in the break room at the squadron when his commanding officer Lieutenant Colonel Ryan came walking in.

"Davis, you have a call from a Diana. She said it's real urgent." Martin stood up. This took him completely by surprise that Diana had called him at work, or that she had called him at all.

"You can take it in the Ready Room." Martin thanked him and hurried to the phone.

"Hello, Diana?" he said with a smile.

"Martin, oh thank God!" she said with a sigh. She sounded hysterical. Martin's smile began to fade.

"Diana, what's wrong?"

"It's Jake. I left him and moved in with Katherine in Las Vegas. He just showed up. He's acting crazy!"

"Did he hit you?" Martin asked with anger.

"No, but he tried. Katherine stopped him. He pushed her against the door and she's out cold. I'm afraid of what he'll do." Martin could hear Jake in the background beating on the door and yelling for her to open up.

"I locked him out of the room, but I don't think that will keep him out for long. Martin, I'm scared!" She began to cry. There was silence on Martin's end.

"Martin, are you there?" she asked.

"Yes, here's what I want you to do. Push a dresser or something very heavy against the door. Does your bedroom have a bathroom?"

"Yes." she said.

"Good, after you've done that, take the phone into the bathroom, lock it, and grab what you can, a razor, or a pair of scissors and keep that with you as a weapon, just in case. You got that?" he asked her.

"Yes." She was very frightened and he knew it. He wished he could come through the phone and save her, but he couldn't. She spoke up.

"If I call the police, the press will show up before they do. Martin, I need you."

"I'll be there as soon as I can. Just keep yourself safe for me until I get there. Now tell me the address." Lieutenant Colonel Ryan looked up from his paperwork and saw Martin storm into his office.

"Sir, I am requesting emergency leave." He said.

"What's the emergency?" the Lieutenant asked.

"You are just going to have to trust me, Sir." Martin told him.

"Well, it must be pretty important for one of my best pilots to request emergency leave. I'll grant it." Martin sighed.

"Oh, thank you, Sir. But there's just one thing."

"What is it, Davis?" Martin was hesitant to respond.

"I'm gonna need a plane, Sir." The Lieutenant's eyes almost popped out when Martin said that.

"You what?"

"Yes Sir. Just a small one"

"Where to?"

"Las Vegas, Sir."

"Absolutely not!"

"Come on Sir, you know me. You know it must be very important for me to ask this of you. I won't let you down. You have my word. I just really need to get to Vegas as fast as possible, Sir." The Lieutenant became silent. He looked down at his desk. What Martin was asking was a lot.

"Sir, I am absolutely desperate to get to Vegas fast. If there were any other way, I would do it, but this is a matter of life and death. You've got to believe me, Sir!" The Lieutenant thought for a moment. He could see the desperation in Martin's eyes. He sighed.

"I have a buddy at the airport off base. I'll see what I can do on such short notice."

"Thank you, Sir!"

"I'll give you twenty-four hours to return it safely or it's your ass, do you understand?" Martin smiled.

"Oh, thank you Sir, I promise that you have nothing to worry about."

"Are you kidding? I have everything to worry about. If you end up wrecking his plane, well, you'll have us both to deal with!"

"I won't let you down, Sir. You have my word."

"Go on and leave before I come to my senses and change my mind. I'll make some phone calls, pull some strings and have a single engine ready for you ASAP. Just don't disappoint me."

"No Sir! Thank you, Sir. See you in twenty-four hours." And with that, Martin ran out of the office.

"Don't let me down." The Lieutenant yelled to Martin as he ran out. Martin took off to his barracks and packed a bag within minutes. Then he headed toward the airport to an awaiting plane. Diana had fallen asleep in the bathroom. She still had the phone in her hand. When she woke, it was quiet. No more pounding on the bedroom door. How long had she been out? she wondered. Probably at least an hour. Maybe Jake had gone, and she could come out. She pulled herself up and stood. It took a few seconds for her to get her balance. She was hungry and her head and eyes ached from crying. She listened for a second and then opened the bathroom door slowly. She peaked around the corner and found her dresser in front of her locked bedroom door, just the way she had left it.

She stood there for a moment wondering if she should move it to see if Jake was still out in the living room waiting for her. She went in the bathroom, grabbed the shears she had been holding onto until she had fallen asleep, and moved the dresser. She stood for a moment and listened. She heard nothing. She then unlocked the bedroom door and slowly opened it. She peeked her head out and didn't see anyone. She opened the door more and stepped out. Lying on the couch was Katherine. She was holding an ice bag over the bump on her head, from when she had hit the door. When she saw Diana, she sat up.

"Are you okay?" Katherine asked her.

"When I came to, Jake was gone, and I couldn't get you to open the bedroom door."

"I was hiding in the bathroom and must have fallen asleep." Diana said.

"Jake is gone?" she asked.

"As far as I know. How are you doing?" Katherine asked her.

"I think I'll be alright. What time is it?"

"4:20pm." Diana sat down on the couch by Katherine. Just then there was a knock at the door. Diana stood up and walked to the door. She put the chain on the door and very slowly opened the door.

"Martin!" But instead of Martin, it was Jake. He put all his weight on the door. The chain gave way and the door broke open.

"Sorry to burst your bubble, sweetie, but it's me." In his hand was a gun. Diana's mouth dropped when she saw the gun. He was pointing it right at her.

"I gave you a chance to come with me on your own, but you refused me. Now, maybe you won't be so stupid." Diana backed slowly away. Katherine stood up and when Jake saw her, he flashed the gun at her. She saw it and jumped back.

"This time, you better just stay out of my way." He said to her.

"Jake, you don't know what you're doing. You need to think about this." Diana was nervous and he could tell it in her voice. It was shaky.

"I have thought about this. All that money I invested in you. You had no right to walk out on me. You're my wife. You're mine." He grabbed her, swung her around and held her in front of him. He put the gun to her head.

"You're coming with me this time." he said. Diana couldn't talk. The barrel of the gun was right on her temple. Jake's back was towards the open doorway. He didn't see Martin coming up from behind. Before Jake new it, Martin grabbed the gun from his hand, swung him around and punched him. Jake hit the floor.

"Didn't your mother ever teach you that you don't hit a lady?" Martin opened up the clip and emptied the magazine, and the bullets fell to the floor. Jake got up.

"Well, look who it is! It's fly-boy. What are you going to do, huh?" Martin was quick to answer.

"I'm gonna give you a little lesson on what I like to call Marine Corps logic. We see a problem, we eliminate it." Jake spoke up.

"I don't think you've got the guts." He lunged toward Martin and swung his fist, but Martin ducked.

"Bad call on your part." He grabbed Jake's arm as it went flying by his head, and swung his arm behind his back. Jake was in tremendous pain. Martin had a tight grip on him so he couldn't move.

"I know you know better than to try anything." Martin said to him.

"Cause if you do, I'll rip your arm right off." Martin pushed Jake up against the wall. He looked over at Diana, who was smiling at him. He smiled at her and gave her a wink. Just then, police officers came into the room.

"This is the trash that needs to go out." Martin said and pushed Jake towards the officers who grabbed his arms and cuffed him. As the police read Jake his rights, Diana ran over to Martin, threw her arms around him and kissed his cheek. He took off his flight jacket and put it around her shoulders. She smiled

"I'm so glad to see you! How did you get here so fast?" He smiled brightly.

"I've got a plane double parked outside." he joked.

Chapter Twelve

After the police hauled Jake off, Martin and Diana took Katherine to the hospital to get her head checked out. Other than a headache, she was fine. Martin decided to take Diana and Katherine out to dinner to get their minds off the day's event. Diana took a shower, and Katherine went to get dressed. Diana put on a blue dress and did her make-up. When she entered the living room, her mouth dropped. Martin was standing in a tux he had quickly run out and rented. He was so handsome, she thought. Just then, Katherine walked in. Seeing how Martin was dressed, she whistled at him. He smiled at her with pride. He looked back at Diana.

"You look beautiful." he said to her.

"Thanks! So do you." she said with a smile.

"Well, shall we go dine?" he asked.

"We shall." she said. They arrived at an Italian restaurant with live entertainment. A pianist was playing. It was Diana's favorite place. As the hostess showed them to their table, Martin told them, "You two order whatever you like, and I'll be right back." When he walked away, Katherine turned to Diana.

"He is sooo handsome! How can you not be melting right now?" she asked Diana. She smiled.

"Katherine, he's just a friend."

"Girl, how can you honestly tell me he's just a friend? I can see it in your eyes. The way they light up when you mention him. The look in your eyes when you saw him come to your rescue. Girl, you've got it bad, you just don't know it." Diana blushed.

"Katherine, you don't know what you're talking about." she said.

"Yes I do. You called him when Jake showed up. You thought about him before anyone else. Girl, you are in denial, and I don't mean a river in Egypt." Diana grinned.

"You're crazy!" she said and tried to stop smiling.

"No, I'm not, and I know he's just as crazy about you. He's got it bad for you." Diana dropped her chin.

"What are you talking about?" she asked.

"Oh, come on. You would have to be blind not to see how he cares about you." said Katherine, matter-of-factly.

"What do you mean?"

"He dropped everything and flew all the way from Camp Pendleton the moment you called him and told him you needed him. If that isn't true love, I don't know what is! I can't even get my boyfriend to get off his lazy butt to come over and help me when the toilet stops up." Diana let out a giggle.

"Besides, his eyes light up when he sees you." Katherine looked up and stopped talking. Martin was walking towards them. He was holding two roses. Katherine leaned in to Diana and whispered.

"You see what I mean? He's got it bad." Martin handed a rose to each of them.

"Two roses for two lovely ladies." he said with a smile. Diana turned to Katherine and gave her a "told you so" look. He offered his arm to Diana.

"May I have this dance?" She smiled up at him.

"If you don't, I will." Katherine said softly. Diana stood up, still holding the rose, and accepted his arm. He walked her to the dance floor. All eyes were on the handsome couple. He held her close to him with no resistance. She moved close to him.

"You're a pretty good dancer." she said to him.

"Thank you, madam." he jokingly said.

"Could you be blushing?" he said to her with a smile. She was.

"Everyone is staring at us." she whispered.

"That's because they envy me. I'm dancing with the most beautiful lady here. Now she was really blushing. She felt all funny inside. What Katherine had said to her about him was spinning in her mind. She was all confused. She didn't know how he was making her feel. Her heart was pounding in her chest.

"Thank you again for saving me from Jake." she said.

"Diana, you know I would do anything for you." he told her.

"You mean the world to me. We're best friends, remember?" Somehow him saying that felt strange to her. Yes, they were best friends, they had always been. But just then, at that moment, after what Katherine had told her and the way they were dancing so close, it felt like much more. They danced around on the dance floor as the slow melody from the piano played on. She smiled, blushing when he looked at her. She felt like a schoolgirl inside.

"So with Jake in his place, when are you going back to LA to live?" he asked. She thought for a moment.

"I have to decide where my home is. I kind of feel like I don't have anything now, like I don't belong anywhere at the moment. My home was with Jake for so long that I'm afraid to be on my own."

"You won't be alone. I'll be nearby. Just call me whenever you need anything. You know I've been known to drop everything and come if ever a friend needs me." he said with a grin. She smiled.

"I really appreciate you coming tonight. I can always count on you, Martin. You're the best friend I've ever had." He should have been flattered at her comment but it still hurt when she pointed out that they were just friends. When the dance was over, they ate dinner and went back to the apartment. When they got inside, it was 10:30 pm. Katherine knew they wanted to be alone.

"Well, it's getting late. I'm going to bed. See you guys in the morning" Katherine said. They said goodnight to her and she went in her room and shut the door, leaving them alone. They stood in the doorway for a moment.

"Would you like to come in for a drink?" she asked.

"No, I better get going to my hotel. I'm flying back tomorrow morning at 10am." She was disappointed. She wanted him to stay a while longer. She told him goodnight and when she reached up to give him a hug, he moved his lips towards her to kiss her. For a moment, she responded and moved her lips toward his. She was feeling weak and didn't know what was happening. Her pulse was racing. Was he kissing her because he does love her, or is he just swept up in the moment too? She was so confused! If she kissed him, what would that do to their friendship? Afraid of messing up their friendship with a kiss, she stopped herself. He was disappointed with her reaction. Knowing that by how she resisted his kiss, she didn't return his love. He knew all he needed to know. He reached down and held her hand.

"If you need me again, here's a better number to reach me at." he said, as he handed her a piece of paper. He kissed her hand and with that, he was gone, leaving her standing alone. Diana sat down on the couch and cried. She was so confused. If she could just make out her feelings, or if she knew if he really loved her, then maybe she could think clearly. The next day, Katherine came out of her bedroom. Diana was sitting at the kitchen table drinking coffee.

"Hey, girl, are you ready to head out to the airport for your flight to Hollywood?" Katherine looked around.

"Where's soldier boy?"

"He's probably on his way to San Diego by now." she said.

"You mean you're letting him go?" Katherine asked with surprise.

"He tried to kiss me last night but I stopped him."

"Are you crazy?"

"Yes. I wanted him to kiss me. But not because he felt pity for me. Poor Diana can't fight her own battles and needs big brother to come fight for her. I don't know. I'm so confused. I don't know what I feel and I don't know how he really feels about me, Katherine. I wish I did. I wish I knew how he truly felt for me. It would make things so much easier. But he's never told me."

"Well, then let me help you." Katherine went over to a drawer and opened it. She pulled out a letter and walked over to Diana.

"The morning of your wedding, I was in the hotel lobby throwing away a coffee cup, and in the trash, I noticed this. I knew it was meant for you when I saw it and so I took it and read it. I was going to give it to you just before the wedding but you were so happy to be marrying Jake then that I didn't want to interfere. But now I think you need to read it. Then you'll know." She handed Diana the letter that Martin had written her the day of her wedding with Jake but had thrown away. Diana looked confused and took the envelope from Katherine. She read the front of the envelope.

"For Diana, please read before you marry Jake." She pulled out the letter inside and read. As she read his letter about how he felt about her she began to cry. When she was done, she looked up at Katherine.

"I never knew." How could I have not known?" A smile came across her face.

"Do you think I could.." Katherine interrupted her.

"He may still be there. If we leave early for your flight, say now, we may catch him." Martin left his hotel room, checked out and took a taxi to the airport. He was depressed that Diana decided she didn't love him. Traffic was jammed and that didn't help his mood very much. Finally, he made it to the airport, and went to the hanger where his rental plane was parked. The maintenance crew was fueling the plane for flight.

"Morning, sir!" a crewman said as he saw Martin approaching.

"Morning." Martin answered back.

"It looks to me like a good day to fly." the man said.

"Sunny sky, not a cloud in sight. The flying conditions are perfect. Can't get any better than that!" Martin looked up at the sky and let out a heavy sigh, and with no expression, he softly said

"Yes, I guess this is as good as it's gonna get."

"I can't believe it. How could I have not seen it? I'm so blind. He felt that way all this time?" Diana was saying as they were driving to the airport.

"You are blind, girl. I knew it the moment I saw him look at you. He's hot, girl. If I were you, I wouldn't let him go for a second. Someone else might snatch him up. Someone like me!" Katherine said. Diana thought for a moment, then yelled, "Why are you talking? Step on it!" Martin stood by his plane as the ground crew was prepping it for flight. He was about to climb up in the cockpit when he turned around and saw Diana walking towards him. He stepped off the ladder and walked to her. Although he was glad to see her, he waited for her to speak. The plane's engine was loud. She had to yell for him to hear her.

"I was wrong when I said I don't have anything. I have you. I've always had you!" He began to smile when he heard this. His heart was pounding.

"Your love for me is more than I've ever deserved." He began to speak, but she interrupted.

"I waited my whole life wondering if you felt the same about me as I did about you! And to think all this time we wasted when we could have been honest with each other from the beginning. It was you, Martin. It was always you! I was just too wrapped up in my career to see it." She walked closer to him and put her hand on his cheek.

"I love you, Martin. I don't want to waste any more time than we've already wasted." A long-awaited smile spread across his face. His eyes began to well up as she spoke the words he had waited to hear for so long.

"Yes!" he yelled looking up in the air. He looked back at her.

"Oh Diana, I have waited so long to hear you say that!" He grabbed her up in his arms, whirled her around, sat her back down and cupped her face with his hands. He pulled her into a deep passionate kiss. He let go of all he was holding back all those years. And she totally gave in to him. Their kiss was the most passionate either one of them had ever felt. As they stood there in their embrace, a tear ran down his cheek. He was filled with so much joy that he couldn't contain it. They slowly pulled away and looked into each other's eyes.

"I was prepared to wait forty years for this, but I'm so glad I don't have to!" She gave him a confused look.

"What?" He just chuckled and said

"Never mind, long story. Remind me to tell you some day." He pulled her into another kiss. After a moment, he pulled away.

"Wait! How did you know?" Diana pulled out the letter. She showed it to him. He was confused.

"Wait! How in the world did you…"

"Katherine found it in the trash the day of my wedding and she kept it all this time. She had a feeling it was something I would need to see when the time was right. She showed me this morning." He looked ashamed.

"I was gonna give it to you that morning, but I didn't want to stop you from…"

"From making the biggest mistake of my life!" she interrupted.

"Martin, I've made some terrible mistakes all my life. But if everything has led up to this moment, then

I'd make them all over again." He smiled and pulled her into another passionate kiss. Just then, Katherine walked up to them.

"Sorry to interrupt this passionate moment, but your plane to L.A. is leaving." she said as she pointed to a plane pulling away from the gate off in the distance. Diana gasped.

"Oh no! What am I gonna do? I have to be at rehearsals in two hours!" Martin thought for a moment.

"Wait right here." he said and walked over to his plane, climbed the ladder, reached in and grabbed his flight jacket. Diana had no idea what he was up to. He walked back to her.

"Since I'm breaking a million rules anyways." He said as he threw his jacket to Diana who quickly caught it.

"What's this for?" she asked.

"Didn't I promise you a ride in a plane once? Now come on, get in." he said with a smile. Her mouth dropped open. She looked at the tiny two-seater single engine plane. She had never been in one so small.

"I can't ride in that. I'm not sure how safe it is." she protested.

"Oh, yes you can, Diana." Katherine interrupted.

"You have an award to accept tonight." Katherine handed Diana the yellow dress she had been carrying in a small bag, along with all her other items she had quickly packed before they headed out towards the airport.

"Here's you dress. Now get going." Katherine said with a smile. Diana looked down at the dress, up at the plane, and back to Katherine.

"Well, I guess I have no other choice, do I?" She asked.

"Nope!" Martin answered as he grabbed her dress and bag and led Diana to the awaiting plane.

"I'll get her there in plenty of time."

"Bye, Diana! I'll be watching. Good luck!" yelled Katherine as she waved.

"Thanks!" Diana yelled back as she was putting the jacket on. Martin was walking her quickly towards the plane.

"I think I'm gonna need it."

Chapter Thirteen

After dropping Diana off at the airport, Martin made it in time to return his plane rental. On his way back to the squadron, he made a quick phone call to the office of the theater where the Music Awards were being held. He had a little surprise in store for Diana. Diana stood behind stage. It was almost time for her to perform. She wished Martin could be there but he had to rush back to base. She really wanted him there with her, but she knew he couldn't. He had given her a kiss and promised he would be watching from his room. She was nervous. She wasn't sure why. She had performed live hundreds of times, but this was the Music Awards. She looked lovely in her yellow dress with her hair done up in ringlets. She knew it wasn't the performance that had her feeling ill, it was something else. She was in love and it was making her feel queasy. Jake never made her feel that way. Backstage, a lady approached Diana with a note in her hand.

"This is for you." the lady said with a smile.

"Thanks." Diana told her and opened the note and read:

"It doesn't matter to me who wins; you've already won my heart. All my love, Martin." She smiled. She took a deep breath and waited to be presented.

"Ladies and gentlemen, the talented Diana Stein." Out in the audience, thousands of people were applauding for her. She walked out and gave a big smile. Cameras were flashing all around her. All the fans that were cheering overwhelmed her! She walked over to her place in front of the microphone. The lights all around dimmed. A hush fell over the crowd. She took a deep breath and smiled.

"I would like to dedicate this song to a dear and special man. He has shown me a love I never knew existed before." She looked up at the camera and smiled.

"Martin, this one is for you." Martin watched from the TV in the Ready Room at the squadron surrounded by Smith, Warren and Green, along with other Marines who were cheering for him. He had a big grin on his face.

"You're one lucky guy!" Smith said as he patted him on the back.

"I know." Martin said with a big grin, his eyes fixed on Diana.

"Very lucky." The music started and she began to sing. It was a beautiful slow ballad. The song was about being lost in the dark and someone showing her that she wasn't alone, that someone was showing her the way. She teared up as she sang. The emotions she felt for Martin overpowered her. When the song was over, the crowd gave her a standing ovation. Martin was full of pride. Diana smiled and told the audience, "Thank you", and blew a kiss, as she walked off stage. She waited backstage as two celebrities came on stage to announce the nominees for best new artist. They named three other artists, but when Diana's name was announced, the audience cheered loudest. Martin, Smith and Green all had their fingers crossed.

"And the winner of best new artist is…." Diana held her breath, so did Martin.

"Miss Diana Stein!" The crowd went wild. Diana almost fell over. She was taken by surprise that she actually won!

"Yesss!" Martin yelled. He, Smith, Green and all the other Marines in the room were cheering. She stood up, walked towards the front and walked up on stage. She was so happy; tears were running down her face. The crowd cheered. She felt like she was in a dream. Slowly, she walked over by the podium. She smiled as she was handed her award. Her hands were shaky as she was in disbelief that she had won. She held it up. She walked up to the microphone and after a moment, the audience hushed.

"Wow, I can't believe this!" She said.

"Thank you so much for voting for me. I can't believe it!" She took a deep breath. She felt like she was walking in the clouds. It all seemed like a dream.

"I want to thank all the people who voted for me and who supported me. My mom, my dad. I love you both. My fans, and to the one above who gave me the gift of song. And last but certainly not least, to the most special person in my life, who is there, who's always been there for me. He saved me in every way imaginable. I wouldn't be here if it wasn't for him, and if it takes the rest of my life, I will devote every second of it showing him how special he is to me. We made promises to each other years ago as kids. He kept his promise to me and now I'm keeping mine." She held up the award and waved it. "Here's to seeing our dreams come true. Martin. I love you." The crowd cheered for her and cameras flashed as she stood holding her trophy.

"I love you too." Martin said softly, as he watched her on the TV.

Chapter Fourteen

The wedding chapel was breathtaking. Beautiful peach and white roses filled the church. Soft music was playing while the guests were taking their seats. Martin stood next to Warren, Smith and Green as they greeted guests walking into the church.

"So now it's your big day, my friend." Warren said as he patted Martin on the shoulder.

"Are you as nervous as I was?"

"No, I'm not nervous, I'm excited. I thought this day would never come."

"Well, you waited forever to win her love and you succeeded." said Green.

"You're the man! We all need lessons from you."

"Thanks." Martin said with a smile.

"LeAnne hunted me down like prey until I gave in. But boy, I'm sure glad I did. She's made me the happiest man in the world." said Smith.

"Ah, the second happiest man." Martin interrupted.

"The happiest man is about to marry the most wonderful woman in the world." Green spoke up.

"See you inside." and the two Marines went in the door. Just then Teresa came up and hugged Martin.

"I'm so happy for you. I knew this day would eventually come."

"Not me, I thought this day would never come." They both smiled. Diana stood in her dressing room looking in the mirror. She was in a lovely wedding gown. It was specially made for her from a top designer from New York. She wanted this day to be the most wonderful day of her life. Her mother Nancy, stood beside her fixing her veil.

"Mom, I think it was fine the way it was before." she said with a smile.

"But it was hiding your beautiful shoulders. You get them from me, you know."

"Yeah, well I must get my nervousness from Daddy. Look at me, I'm shaking so badly." Diana held up her hands to show them trembling.

"I hope it's just stage fright and not cold feet making you nervous." her mother said.

"Oh, it nerves! This is nothing like it was with Jake. I love Martin so much I can't stand it. I'm walking down the aisle to marry the handsome prince and I couldn't be happier, but I also couldn't be more nervous." She let out a big sigh.

"Mom, how did you ever get through it twice?"

"It was hard the first time. I loved your father so much that I thought I was going to die, and when we got back together and remarried last month, I felt like the same shaking young bride all over again." They both giggled.

"But I knew both times going in that he was the one I wanted to be with forever. And now we both know that we are going to make it work this time. Just like I know that you and Martin are going to make it. He loves you so much. He would do anything for you, he always has. That kind of love doesn't just go away. You'll see." There was a knock on the door and it opened.

"Diana, it's time." her father said as he peeked into the room. She turned to her mother and they exchanged smiles and hugged.

"Go get em, tiger." her mom said. Diana turned and walked towards her father, took his arm and walked to where they were to stand to get ready to walk down the aisle. The wedding march began and she and her father exchanged smiles.

"Are you ready sweetheart?" her father asked.

"Never been more ready for anything in my life!" The doors opened. The wedding march began playing. Martin stood at the altar waiting nervously. When he saw her, his heart skipped a beat. He had never seen her look so beautiful. She was stunning! He never took his eyes off her as she walked slowly towards him. She smiled as she saw him and kept her gaze fixed on his face. She was walking down the aisle and this time it was for him. Life couldn't be better. When she reached him, her father gave her a kiss on the hand and she went to stand next to her groom. The minister began the ceremony and Martin and Diana stood hand and hand. They had written their own vows and when it was Martin's turn, he turned towards Diana and began.

"I, Martin, take thee Diana, for my wife. I promise to love and cherish you just as I have most of my life. You are everything to me and my heart is only half without you. You deserve the best and that is what I promise to you. You never have to worry about my love for you ever dying; because it grows stronger every moment, every second when I'm with you. I love you, Diana. More than any man has ever loved a woman. This I promise you now and forever; and nothing in this world means more to me than this moment." He turned to Warren, who was his best man.

"You got the rings, man?" Warren patted at his pockets and got a worried look on his face. Martin's eyes began to get wide. Warren reached in a pocket and after a long pause, pulled out the rings.

"Just kidding." Martin pushed him jokingly with his elbow and took one ring. He reached for Diana's hand and held it in his. He began slipping the ring on her finger.

"With this ring, I promise to cherish you now, and as always, until the end of time." He pushed the ring up onto her finger and kissed her hand. They both smiled. It was Diana's turn. She gave Katherine her bouquet to hold. Then she turned to him.

"I, Diana, take thee Martin, as my husband. I promise to love and cherish you for all my life. You have been there for me when no one else seemed to be. You have taught me what true friendship and true love really is. My heart is only half without you. No woman could ever be as happy as I am right now. I love you, Martin. And I promise to love you now and forever." She took the remaining ring from Warren, and began slipping it on Martin's finger.

"With this ring, I promise to cherish you now and until the end of time." She finished slipping his ring on and smiled at Martin. A tear rolled down her cheek. The minister began to talk again and they turned to face him.

"If anyone here feels that this couple should not be wed, speak now or forever hold your peace." Warren turned to the audience.

"No one better say a word!" Everyone laughed. The minister continued.

"With the power vested in me by the state of California, I now pronounce you husband and wife. You may now kiss the bride." Martin faced Diana. He lifted the veil from her face and over her head.

"You bet I will." She giggled and they kissed. Everyone began to applaud. Some of Martin's Marine buddies stood up, whooping and hollering.

"Alright Davis, way to go!" Marines stood in formation along the isle, holding up swords. Warren stood at the end and when Martin and Diana walked through, Warren swatted his sword on Diana's behind, which was a Marine wedding tradition. It surprised her. She gasped and then smiled. Everyone gathered outside and waited for Diana to throw the bouquet. Single women bunched up to try and catch it. Diana turned around and threw it. It sailed up in the air and a group of hands went to grab it. It was a mess. Arms were everywhere. Women were giggling and screaming. Smith turned to Warren.

"Man, it's like a bunch of hungry birds fighting over a crumb." Warren laughed. When the commotion was over, Katherine was left holding the bouquet, jumping up and down.

"I got it. I got it!" Smith, who was in his uniform walked up to Katherine.

"Need an escort to the reception?" he asked while holding out his elbow to her. She smiled and grabbed it. "Yes, that would be great." She turned to Diana and winked at her. Diana giggled. Everyone gathered at the squadron hanger for the reception. All the jets were moved outside and flowers and streamers were everywhere. A band was set up and a dance area was out in front of the band. Diana and Martin danced out on the dance floor. His Marine buddies were dancing with thier women by them; including Katherine and Smith, James and Nancy. Martin held Diana close, looking into her eyes.

"You know you've made me the happiest man today. I don't think I could get much happier." he said to her softly.

"I hope that's not true because, Martin, there's something I want to tell you. I wanted to wait until we were married before I did." she replied.

"Yes?"

"Well, next time you take me up in a plane, you better make it a three-seater." she teased.

"Why?"

"Well, because there's a little co-pilot on his way in about six months." Martin's jaw dropped.

"You mean?"

"We're gonna have a baby." she said. A smile grew across his face.

"Are you serious?" She smiled and nodded her head.

"I'm gonna be a daddy?" Again, she nodded. He leaned down and kissed her. He ran his hand along her belly. He was wrong to think that he couldn't get any happier, because she just made him even more so.

"I love you so much, Diana."

"I love you too."

Chapter Fifteen

F ive months later Diana sat in a chair with her face towards the sky. It was the annual Beaufort air show and she, along with Martin, Warren, LeAnne, Katherine, Smith and Green had flown in from Camp Pendleton to attend the air show where Martin and his buddies Smith and Green were flying their jets in the show. Martin kissed her goodbye as he rubbed his hand over her baby belly, which had gotten quite big. She wished him good luck. LeAnne and Katherine sat next to Diana. Warren, Green and Smith were saying goodbye to them before their flight.

"I'll be watching for you." Diana said with a smile.

"Now don't go into labor while we're up there." Warren said jokingly to Diana.

"We'll only be an hour or so," Martin told her.

"Okay." Diana, Katherine and LeAnne kissed their husbands goodbye. They waited and watched for the men to fly by in their planes. Later, when Diana saw Martin and Warren's jet, she smiled excitedly. Their jet did turns and belly rolls. They came close to other jets, and it looked like they would collide. But it was part of the show to add suspense. Watching it made Diana feel nervous. She got a little short winded. She wasn't used to the allergies and weather of Beaufort, and was a little nervous about being back, but she wanted to be there, back in her old hometown.

"It's alright, Diana, it's just part of the show." LeAnne tried to comfort her.

"They have practiced hundreds of times." They did some more flying and were getting even closer to the other jets. She got even more nervous. She found herself having trouble breathing. She was wheezing more and more. She soon found she could hardly breathe. LeAnne and Katherine noticed her struggling for air and helped her up to her feet.

"It's okay Diana, calm down." Katherine said. But Diana couldn't breathe. LeAnne held her arm and walked her over to the medical team that was there just in case there were any mishaps. Seeing that Diana was in bad shape, the paramedics decided to rush her to the hospital. Katherine and LeAnne stayed behind and made sure Martin was made aware of the situation as soon as he landed. He knew how bad her asthma attacks were. Worried out of his mind, he rushed to the hospital as fast as he could possibly go. As he drove, he prayed harder than he ever had before.

Chapter Sixteen

Holding the old photo of Diana that he always carried with him, Martin sat in the waiting room. It had been a few hours since she was taken to the ER. He was surrounded by his friends and his mother. It seemed like forever since he heard anything from the doctor on how Diana's condition was. He was informed that she was placed on a ventilator. James and Nancy had just arrived and walked briskly over to Martin.

"Have you gotten to see her yet?" James asked.

"No, not yet." Just then, Dr. Peterson approach.

"Mr. Davis, Diana is stable for the moment. But there is a lot of scar tissue in her lungs due to the pulmonary fibrosis and her airways are quite blocked. We recommend we do a lung transplant."

"Wait! Pulmonary fibrosis? She just has asthma." Martin was confused.

"Mr. Davis, she was diagnosed with pulmonary fibrosis about four months ago according to her medical file.

"What?" Everyone was quickly confused.

"Sometimes it can go undiagnosed because the symptoms can be identical to asthma."

"Why wouldn't she tell me any of this? I'm her husband! I'd have supported her. I'd have made her do treatment!"

"Mr. Davis, she was offered medication, but refused. She didn't want to harm the baby."

"She's always been stubborn." James said with tears in his eyes.

"I can't believe she kept it from me. I would have insisted she take the treatment!" Martin was in shock.

"That is why she probably didn't say anything." Nancy added.

"She didn't want to lose the baby!" Dr. Peterson spoke up.

"She's still under the effects of the anesthesia so she isn't awake yet. We won't know for sure how she is going to do until she wakes up. I'm afraid she's going to be on the ventilator until she can breathe on her own. You have to consider the possibility that she won't' be able to. We are being optimistic, but to be honest, this was a lot on her system. She's stable at the moment, but only time will tell how she's going to pull through this. We'll get you in to see your wife as soon as we can." Martin looked up at him. His eyes were puffy from crying.

"Thank you." he said very weakly."

"Mr. Davis, we will need an answer on the transplant quickly. I'll give you a few minutes to talk it over with her parents. There is a donor 12 miles away who is a match. But we need to act quickly." Martin nodded.

"When can I see my son?"

"I'll send a nurse to take you back in a few minutes." Dr. Peterson headed out of the room.

"Okay, thank you!" Martin didn't know what to do. A transplant was such a risky procedure. What if she doesn't make it? What if she doesn't have the operation and ends up having another attack when no one is around? He was struggling with the decision.

"What do you both think?" He asked James and Nancy.

"We have the same fears you do. But I think her best option would be the transplant." Said James.

"I think so, too" Nancy said sobbing. She was trying to hold back her tears.

"It's so risky either way. She's been through so much with struggling to breathe for so long. But as her husband, I think it's gonna have to be your call." Just then a nurse came up.

"Would you like to see your son?"

"Oh yes please!" The nurse saw that Martin had a large group of people with him and spoke up.

"I'm sorry, but only immediate family can go in." Martin looked over at his friends. Katherine put her hand on Martin's shoulder.

"We'll wait here. Go meet your son." He smiled at her, put his hand over hers and thanked her. He, his mother, James and Nancy, followed the doctor to the nursery while the rest of the group stayed in the waiting room. When Martin walked in the nursery, he looked down at his newborn son lying in an incubator hooked up to tubes. He was so tiny. He couldn't help but smile a little when he saw him.

"He's beautiful, like his mother." Martin said through his tears.

"He's very beautiful." James said.

"You should be proud." Martin looked up from his baby and to James.

"Thank you." he said with a small smile.

"I'm sorry you can't hold him just yet." said the nurse.

"He's still too weak." Martin looked back at his son.

"Hi little guy I'm Daddy." he said to him.

"I'm gonna take real good care of you." He was having trouble holding his voice strong. He was overwhelmed by his emotions.

"So, what are you going to name him?" asked Teresa. Martin looked up at her and down at his son. He thought for a moment, then looked up and smiled.

"Well, Diana and I had picked out a name. Michael. So that's what it will be. Mike for short." Teresa smiled and nodded.

"That's perfect. He would have liked that" He looked down at his baby and smiled.

"Hello Michael, welcome to the world."

For a moment, Martin thought he witnessed a small smile on his newborn son's face. A moment later, Doctor Peterson came in the room.

"You can see your wife now." Martin walked slowly into Diana's hospital room. It was dark from the shade on the window being closed. He saw his wife lying peacefully still in the bed. She was hooked up to monitors, tubes and wires keeping her vitals monitored. The Ventilator was in her mouth. She looked rough. It made him so sad to see her like that. Martin walked over and stood by her bed. Tears ran down his cheek as he looked down at his wife. He squatted down beside her. He brushed his hand across her cheek

"You look so beautiful and peaceful, Diana. Our son Michael is just as beautiful as you are. I know you would think so too if you could see him. You've made me so happy by giving me this precious son." He picked up her hand and held it in his.

"Why didn't you tell me Diana? I could have helped you through this!? Oh, Diana. What do I do? I wish you could tell me what you want. I don't want you to suffer any more. How do I make this decision without you?" For a long moment, he just looked at her. He leaned over and kissed her on the lips.

"I love you, Diana." Dr Peterson interrupted.

"Mr. Davis, I'm sorry but it's time. We need an answer now."

Epilogue

Martin stood in the cemetery looking down at the tombstone. He had been hesitant to come visit for a while, too scared of the pain it would bring him. He looked around him as he stood. It was a peaceful sunny summer day. Teresa was a few feet behind Martin. He stood there for a while before he got the strength to speak. Finally, he spoke up.

"Hi, I guess you have been expecting me. Sorry it took so long for me to get the courage up to come here. The pain of losing you is too hard to handle"

Martin started to cry. He wiped away the tears and got his composure and continued.

"You were taken away from me so suddenly that nothing makes sense to me. Knowing that I will never get to see you again. Words can't describe the pain of knowing that." Tears fell and he wiped them away.

"Every moment I had with you was such a blessing to me. Nothing could ever take the place of you. I really needed you and I will always need you. Even though you aren't here physically, I know I will always feel you here with me, watching over me." He looked back at Teresa who wiped a tear from her eye and reached up to put a hand on his shoulder. Martin looked back at her and they shared a tiny smile through the pain. He looked down at the flowers he had been holding in his hand. He bent down to put the flowers on his father's grave.

"I love you Dad!" Martin stood up and Teresa put an arm around his shoulders. He was so thankful his mom had come out to California to help him say goodbye to his dad and to help Diana with the baby while she recovered. Teresa turned and headed toward the car where Diana was sitting in the passenger seat holding baby Mike as she was waiting for them. Diana was still a bit weak from the lung transplant she had gotten a month ago and was still taking it easy.

"I hope you and your father had a nice visit. Are you okay?" she asked as Martin climbed into the driver's seat. Teresa took Mike from Diana and put him in the car seat in the back. He looked at his beautiful wife, at Michael who was sleeping in his car seat and smiled, feeling very blessed at what God had given him.

"Yes! I couldn't be better!"

About The Author

Julie has always had a passion for writing. As a young child, she wanted to be a writer. She is the daughter of an Air Force veteran. Her family moved around a lot and she was in a new school almost every year. Writing kept her grounded. At the age of 19 she married her high school sweetheart and moved to California where he was stationed in the Marine Corps. The military has always been a part of her life and is a huge influence on her writing. She lives in Florida with her husband of 28 years. They have a daughter in college. Her family is very important to Julie and they continue to inspire her every day.